Kisses, Kayaks & Monsters

Ashleigh Stevens

KISSES, KAYAKS, & MONSTERS
First edition. JULY 1, 2021

Edited by

www.WIPWonders.com

Other Works by Ashleigh Stevens

Becoming Birgit

Boarding School Blues

Camp Piquaqua

Hartfield Chronicles

Mooncrossed

One Night In Sedona
(writing as Carrie Latimer)

To receive updates on new releases,
join my newsletter or visit
www.AshleighsStevensBSB.com.

Chapter 1

I rushed down the hall of the science center, checking the colorful labels on the side of each door. Professor Larkin hadn't actually told me where to find his office. The biology department was spread out over three levels. Was I even on the right floor? I really needed this summer internship and showing up five minutes late for my interview was not a good way to start.

Thankfully, I found the office without too much trouble. I quickly rapped on the closed door, glancing at my watch. Only two minutes late. Hopefully, Larkin's clock was slow.

"Come in!"

I opened the door and stuck my head inside. "Professor Larkin? I'm Ellie Bassett. I'm here about the summer internship?"

He nodded, gesturing toward one of the wooden armchairs in front of his desk. "Please, come in. Close the door."

I glanced around the room as I followed his instructions. His computer sat in one corner of a U-shaped desk so full of books and papers, I wasn't sure how he could even find his keyboard. Behind him, a window overlooked the courtyard, with a glimpse of the Elver River down the hill. To my right, books were arranged in neat rows on their shelves. A quick glance at the titles showed they were mostly textbooks. Built into the wall on my left, above the professor's head, were bookshelves filled with thinner books that seemed to focus on specific aspects of marine biology. Beneath the shelf, a grey bulletin board was covered with pictures of maps and what looked to be a kindergartner's illustration of a dinosaur.

Professor Larkin looked away from his computer as I took my seat. He was one of the younger members of the faculty, still working toward his tenure. His brown hair was just a little too long, swept to the side. Combined with the stubble around his chin and the oxford shirt, he looked ready to go sailing in a yacht, not give a ninety-minute lecture about the chemical makeup of water.

He smiled at me, his teeth nearly pearlescent enough to reflect the sunlight. "Ellie. Glad to meet you. So, tell me. How did you learn about this internship?"

I shrugged. "I saw a flier on the bulletin board near the biology lecture hall."

"And what do you know about the position?"

"Nothing, really. I was hoping you could tell me more."

He nodded and leaned back in his chair, steepling his hands in front of him. "I have been commissioned to create bathymetric maps of the Elver River from the Connecticut border to Long Island Sound. I'm looking for two interns to perform that task for me this summer."

I held up my phone. "Do you mind if I write a few things down?"

"By all means."

I typed *bathymetric* as Professor Larkin described the history of the river, focusing more on the indigenous people and early settlers than the water itself. I really had no idea what any of it had to do with marine biology, but I took notes until he was done. From what I gathered, he was looking for two people to kayak along the river all summer. And he was going to pay them for it. That was all I needed to know.

He sent me that blinding smile again. "So, does that sound interesting to you?"

I nodded. "Definitely."

"Great. So, a few quick questions. In your email, you mentioned you were a biology major. Pre-med?"

"Ye—No." At Professor Larkin's raised eyebrows, I sighed. "I was pre-med, but my biology grades my first year weren't that great and the advisor suggested maybe I consider something else. I'm still biology with a pre-med concentration, but I'm not sure what I'm going to do with it yet."

"So, what happened freshman year? Was it just the adjustment to college? Learning how to study?"

I shook my head. "No. My other grades were fine. It's just . . . I don't want to speak ill of any professor."

"Our Introduction to Biology professors change every semester. I am not going to look to see which one you had three years ago. I promise, you can speak freely."

I gave a resigned sigh. "Well, so, you just told me all about the river and how most people think the Vikings named it, but it could have been the French or the English or even the indigenous tribes. On a test, if you asked *How did the river get its name*, I would expect that to be like, a short answer question. But, my biology teacher would make that multiple choice where Vikings was the right answer because it was what the majority of people thought, even though current research is suggesting it might be, whatever. A different answer."

Professor Larkin nodded. "I see. And have you done better in subsequent biology classes?"

"Yeah. But, it took me too long in that first class to bring up my grades. And, well, I'm just not sure about medical school anymore."

"And, what about your boating skills?"

"What about them?"

He gave a small laugh. "Can you row a kayak?"

"Oh. Yeah, sure." I had no idea, but it looked easy enough.

"And you can swim?"

I nodded. "Of course." So, maybe I wasn't the *best* swimmer, but I planned on rowing with a life jacket and I knew how to paddle my way back to shore.

"How do you feel about camping?"

I smiled. "I love it. My family and I go every other weekend all summer."

"Fantastic. Now, let's talk technology. Have you ever seen one of these before?"

He passed me a tablet with buttons on the side. It wasn't powered on and I had no idea how to do so. I hoped my technological ignorance wouldn't hinder my prospects.

I returned the device to him. "It looks like some sort of gaming system."

To my relief, he smiled. "It's a chartplotter. It's used to create the maps." He pressed a button. When the screen lit up, he returned the tablet to me.

"Do me a favor? Do you think you can find the feature to create a new map?"

Typical professor. Giving me a pop quiz on my interview. I might as well walk out now. There was no way I was going to get this job. But, I would humor him.

It took more time than I would have liked. After a few attempts, I grew resolute. I no longer cared about the job. I was not going to leave that office until I learned how to create a new map.

Finally, I figured it out. With a proud smile, I returned the chartplotter and glanced at the clock. Although it had felt like hours, the process had taken only a few minutes.

Professor Larkin nodded. "Very good. Thank you. Well, I'm interviewing a few more people during the week, but you should plan on hearing from me by Monday."

He reached across the table and shook my hand. Rising, I made my way to the door. I was about to turn the knob when Professor Larkin called out to me.

"Oh, one more thing. What are your thoughts on Elver?"

I shrugged. "It's a nice river. Has a tendency to flood the *Elver Ale* every spring."

I was a little annoyed when he laughed. I wasn't trying to be funny, but it seemed he was expecting a different answer.

Kayleigh was sitting in our living room when I entered our apartment. "How was the interview?"

Tossing my keys in the basket beside the front door, I shook my head. "Where's that application for Barney's Burgers?"

"That bad, huh?"

"You better brace yourself for the fact that I may not be able to save up enough for next year's rent." I sat in the chair opposite my roommate and recounted my afternoon. She laughed when I told her my response to Professor Larkin's final question.

I flopped back with a sigh. "You too? Why is that so funny?"

Kayleigh shook her head. "Not uh. I'm not going to ruin the surprise for you. Come on. We're going to be late, and I know what song I'm singing."

Although technically the *Elver Ale House* was a restaurant, it was voted the number one bar in the area every year. The food and the beer were so cheap, it was always crowded.

Especially on Thursdays. Karaoke night. Kayleigh and I had discovered this by accident on her twenty-first birthday, nearly four months ago, and had been visiting every week since.

Kayleigh and I ordered drinks at the bar, greeting various

classmates on our way. While my roommate debated with someone I had never met about the hidden meaning behind one of the books they were reading in Modern Lit, I scanned the room for a table while listening to a very off-key showtune.

"Looking for someone?"

I turned back to the bar. Kayleigh had been absorbed into the crowd, replaced by a guy I had seen in the hallways. I was pretty sure he was another biology major, but we had never actually met. He wore jeans and a shirt just tight enough to show off some impressive abdominal muscles. Like many of my classmates this semesters, he was sporting that unshaven look I found wildly attractive. White sunglasses sat in his buzzed hair, freeing his dark eyes to smile at me. I tried to find my voice.

"Oh. Uh, no. I was just, uh, looking for a table."

"Well, in that case—" He took my hand, dragging me across the floor. While I was flattered by the attention, and hoping to get to know this guy a little better, I wasn't sure how comfortable I was with his forwardness. I searched for Kayleigh as he brought me to to the back of the room, just far enough from the karaoke stage that I could hear myself think.

The guy gestured to an abandoned high top with several dirty plates and pint glasses stacked in the center. "This one just opened up." He took a seat as a waitress came to clear the table.

I bit my lower lip. "I don't know. I'm here with a friend."

He pointed to an extra seat. "Your friend can join us."

"Fine." Shaking my head, I sat across from him.

"Clay." He held up his drink.

I clinked my glass to his bottle. "Ellie."

"So, what brings you here on this lovely evening?"

"My roommate and I come for karaoke night every week."

"This is a weekly thing? Note to self: stay away from Elver Ale on Thursdays."

I giggled. "It's not so bad. There's this one guy, I think he's a history professor. Does a great job with children's songs."

Clay groaned. "Seriously?"

"No. I mean, like, songs from children's movies."

Clay sent me an unconvinced smile, pointing to my glass. "That smells good. What is it?"

"It's called *el cafecito*. Coffee liqueur, rum, and I have no idea what else." I took a large swig.

"You might want to slow down on that."

I shook my head. "I just had the worst job interview ever. I'm treating myself to an extra drink tonight. And a big plate of nachos."

"That's too bad. About the interview. The nachos actually sound like a good idea. Be right back."

He disappeared into the crowd before I could say anything. I drained my glass and contemplated another. While I was still deciding, Kayleigh joined me.

"Found you. Okay. I put my name in."

"Great. What're you singing?"

"It's a sur—"

Kayleigh cut herself off when Clay returned to his seat, passing me a glass of the same cocktail I had just downed. She sent me a look that clearly asked what was going on. I smiled and gestured across the table.

"Clay, this is my roommate, Kayleigh. Kayleigh, this is Clay."

"Nice to meet you." He sent her a smile, but I noticed he didn't offer to clink glasses with her. I tried not to read too much into it. "Did you have a horrible interview as well?"

Kayleigh smiled. "No. I'm interning at the same publishing house I did last year. How about you? Do you have a job lined up for the summer?"

Clay smiled. "Almost. Talked to one of my professors yesterday. He more or less offered me a job working with him on his research project. He just has to finish the interviews and make everything final."

"That's great."

A waitress approached with a plate of nachos as the song ended. The emcee took the microphone.

"Kayleigh Roberts?"

"Ooh. I'm up. It was nice to meet you. I'll catch up with you later, Elle."

With a wink in my direction, Kayleigh hopped off her stool and melted into the crowd. A moment later, she was standing in the front of the room, singing a song I didn't recognize.

"Your friend's pretty good." Clay gestured to the front of the room with a nacho.

I nodded, but didn't respond. Kayleigh usually liked to sing pop hits, but this was some sort of Halloween song about monsters. I had no idea if she was on key, but everyone clapped loudly when she was done, so I assumed she did a good job.

"Hey. I need to hit the men's room. Save my seat."

I turned my attention back to Clay, who was already leaving the table.

"Huh? Yeah. Sure."

As I watched him head off to the men's room, my eyes landed on some of the black and white photographs decorating the walls. Since the restaurant was located next door to the university's boat launch, there were many images of the school's rowing teams from the past hundred or so years. Mixed among them were pictures of fishing vessels and the old steamers used to transport goods up and down the river ages ago.

However, the faded article just behind Clay's seat was the one that caught my eye. The cartoon dinosaur was nearly identical to the one I had seen on Professor Larkin's wall. But, that wasn't what drew my attention. It was the headline.

Elver: The River Monster Returns

Chapter 2

Despite three years at Elver University, I had never stepped foot in the school pool. I hadn't even been aware there *was* one until my sophomore year boyfriend mentioned he was on the swim team. Since we were only together a few weeks, I never had a chance to attend one of his meets.

I reached the fitness center with plenty of time before I was expected to meet Professor Larkin. I smiled at the person behind the desk as I scanned my ID.

"Hi. I'm looking for the pool, but I'm not sure how to get there."

The girl glanced up from the book she was highlighting to point behind me. "It's about a mile up Cross Street, near the tennis courts. You can park in Lot Q." Her voice and expression were so deadpan, that for a moment I almost believed her.

I smiled. "That's funny."

She raised her eyebrows. "What is?"

"Never mind." I shook my head as I quickly made my way to the locker room. Sitting on a bench, I pulled up a campus map on my phone and quickly scanned for the pool. The girl at the desk wasn't lying. The natatorium was almost a mile away.

I raced out of the building to the bus stop. The campus shuttle was just pulling away. Groaning, I headed toward the pool on foot. One mile uphill was going to make me late for my first day at work.

I was still amazed that I had managed to impress Professor Larkin. Relieved, of course, that I had landed a paid internship, but definitely surprised. Apparently, he thought my camping experience would work nicely with the rowing experience of my new coworker.

Someone on the university crew team.

I was sweaty and panting when I finally stepped onto the deck. After stopping for a quick sip at the water fountain, my breathing returned to normal as I looked around. The pool was larger than I had expected, but there were no buoys to denote lanes. Two boats sat in the far corner. Beside them, two men were speaking with their backs to me.

Professor Larkin looked toward me as I made my way across the deck.

"Ah, Miss Bassett. Glad you could make it."

"Sorry I'm late." I could feel my face grow warm and hoped everyone would attribute it to the temperature of the room.

Professor Larkin shook his head. "Not a problem. Have you met Mr. Marris?"

I followed his gaze to the guy standing beside him. I could feel my face grow even warmer as Clay smiled at me.

"El cafecito."

I gave a small wave. I was going to be spending my summer with Clay? After our meeting at the Elver Ale last week, we had been exchanging waves when we passed each other on campus. But now I would be working and living with him for the next two months? I wasn't quite sure how I felt about this sudden development.

But, Professor Larkin didn't give me any time for introspection. "Oh, good. You know each other. So, before the semester ends, I wanted you two to get yourselves familiar with the chartplotter. But first, I thought you should probably row together."

He gestured toward a yellow kayak with two seats. Two paddles rested beside it. I sent him a curious look.

"Um, how are we going to bring that down to the river?" He didn't expect us to carry it three miles downhill, did he?

Professor Larkin waved a dismissive hand. "It fits in the bed of my truck. But, today, we're staying in the pool."

Clay raised his eyebrows. "So, we're rowing a kayak in a pool?" I could tell by his tone he found this notion as crazy as I did.

Professor Larkin laughed. "It's a lot easier to rescue you, and the boats, in the pool." He raised his eyebrows at me. "Where's your life jacket?"

"I don't have one."

He frowned, but Clay spoke before he could. "I brought both of mine. I think one will fit you."

"Thanks."

Professor Larkin nodded. "You're going to want to grab your own by the time we set out next month. The sporting goods store on Main Street should have some."

Clay nodded. "That's where I got mine." He shrugged on a red life jacket as he passed me a yellow one.

There was a bench in front of one of the windows. I placed my bag on it, then kicked off my sandals and stripped off my shirt to reveal my bathing suit. The life jacket was a little large for me to use all summer, but it was comfortable enough to wear for the day.

Professor Larkin pointed to the ramp as I returned to the boat. "Most of the time, you will be placing the boat in the water along the shore. You won't have docks. So, I thought you should practice getting in and out on the ramps."

Clay bent down and grabbed a string at the front of the boat before glancing at me. From his expectant look, I realized he wanted me to grab the other end. I tried not to sigh as I did.

Clay nodded. "On three. One. Two. Three."

He counted so fast, I didn't fully register what he wanted me to do. As he lifted the kayak, it dawned on me that we were carrying it to the ramp. I hefted my end and followed him to the edge of the pool. He waded in until the water was about halfway to his knees before setting down the boat, pushing it forward as I stepped onto the ramp.

It wasn't very wide. It was a tight squeeze standing beside it with the boat. I frowned at Clay.

"Now what?"

"I'm . . . not sure. I've never gotten in a boat from the water before."

Professor Larkin clapped his hands once. "Okay. I'm going to let you two work that out. Clay has the checklist of things you need to work on before you're done. I'll be back in two hours to check your progress."

Without waiting for a reply, Professor Larkin walked out of the room. I turned my attention back to Clay. He was frowning at the boat.

"I think we did this wrong. You aren't over 150 pounds, are you?"

I put my hands on my hips. "Excuse me?"

Clay smiled at me. "Sorry. That came out wrong. I meant, I weigh about 150. If you're heavier than me, you should probably be in the back."

I folded my arms across my chest. "I'm not."

"Yeah, I didn't think so. Okay. So, we need to change spots. Actually, you're good. Just, hold the boat steady while I climb in."

I was still holding my little handle. As Clay came to stand beside me, I put my other hand behind the opening of his seat. He placed his hand near mine and grabbed the side of the boat with his other before smiling at me.

"Ready?"

"For what?" I was having a little trouble focusing with Clay so close to me.

"For me to climb in?"

I didn't miss the incredulity in his tone. He probably thought I was an idiot. I nodded. "Yeah. I guess so."

I watched him push with his arms as if he were trying to lift himself out of the pool. He easily swung one leg in, then the other, and settled into his little seat before flashing me a smile.

"Easy peasy. Alright. Pass me a paddle and I'll turn the boat around so you can try."

I went back to where we had found the boat and grabbed both paddles, glad he remembered them before we were both in the kayak. After I passed him one, he gestured for the other. "Might as well give me yours, too. You'll need it in a minute."

I nodded and passed him the second one. He stowed it between himself and the side of the boat before placing the blade of his paddle against the pool wall. With a push, he coasted out of the ramp. I watched him paddle the kayak toward the center of the pool, turn around, and coast back into the ramp. I stopped the boat with my hand as it approached. He smiled at me.

"Okay. Your turn."

I placed one hand on the side of the boat and the other on the front. I tried to push myself like Clay had done, but ended up toppling head-first into the boat. Clay's laughter echoed across the pool. I was mortified. I quickly moved my hands to grab the opposite side, pulling the rest of my body into the boat. Once my knees were in, I scooted around until I was facing forward. I could again feel the blood rushing to my face. I didn't dare look at Clay.

Something tapped my shoulder. I glanced down to see the blade of a paddle. I mumbled as I took it from Clay.

"Thanks."

"That wasn't so bad. Okay. Now, use the paddle to push us off the wall. The next item on our checklist is to paddle across the pool together."

As we coasted backwards, I could hear some clacking on the

side of the boat. I turned around.

"What was that noise?"

Clay reached to one of his feet. "I'm adjusting the pedals. You definitely need to."

"I thought we rowed with the oars."

He shook his head. "You've never been in a kayak before, have you?"

I rolled my lips inward. Thankfully, Clay just smiled. "It's easy. So, first, you want to bring the pedals up so your knee is resting along the side like this. Just squeeze the little tab and move it toward you."

He demonstrated. It looked easy enough. Except, my pedals were so far in the front of the boat, I couldn't reach them. I had to scoot off my seat to grab the first one. While I was there, I moved the second one.

I settled myself in my chair and adjusted the pedals. Satisfied, I turned my head back around.

"Okay. Now what?"

"Now, we go grab your paddle."

I looked around. I had placed it across the boat in front of me, but with all the pedal adjustments, it must have fallen off. It was drifting in the center of the pool. I groaned, but Clay laughed.

"It's not a big deal. I'm glad we're not in the river. I guess Larkin expected something like this."

With a couple of strokes, he rowed alongside my paddle. I reached over, careful not to fall out as I grabbed it and pulled it back aboard.

"Got it."

"Great. So, I'm going to take a wild guess that you don't have a lot of experience with this and I'm going to give you a few hints. Humor me. You want to hold your paddle like this."

He held his in front of him as he proceeded to spend the next five minutes telling me where to hold the shaft, how to align my knuckles, and how hard I should grip the thing. Finally, I dipped the paddle into the water and the boat began to move.

We traveled across the pool in a zigzag motion until we reached the far wall. There, we managed to turn the boat around and row in a straight line to the opposite wall. I started to angle the kayak for another lap, but Clay stopped me when we were parallel to the edge of the pool.

"Hang on. I have an idea. Pick up your paddle."

When I did as instructed, he used his own to reach the pool

deck and pull us closer to the wall. When he could grab it with his hand, he gave a push, coasting us into the side of the ramp. I reached up to grasp the rail as the front of the boat nearly collided with the wall. I turned around in my seat.

"What'd you do that for?"

Clay had already placed his paddle on the deck and was climbing out of the boat. "I need to grab a few things. Just hold on."

Since I had a feeling he meant literally, I didn't let go of the rail. Clay went to grab the second boat, which was basically an inflatable raft a little shorter than our kayak and twice as wide. A carabiner was attached to a rope tied to the front. After placing the new boat in the water behind the kayak, Clay clipped it to the handle and climbed back into his seat.

"So, each morning, we have to pack up camp and stow everything into this raft, then drag it downstream. Larkin wants us to practice rowing with it."

I shook my head. "Whatever."

After a few laps towing the boat, Clay decided we were in tune enough to try mapping. He once again docked under the rail and removed the raft. The chartplotter boat was a lot smaller, not much bigger than a shoebox, with the sonar device installed in the bottom. After clipping it to the back of the kayak, Clay passed me the transponder and returned to his seat.

"Larkin said we had to map the entire pool twice each. So, you get to play with it first while I row."

With a shrug, I tried to remember how I had set up the map during my interview last week. I did it in less than a minute.

"All set."

"Perfect." Clay pushed us away from the wall, turning us to row across the pool. After two laps, I swapped the transponder for the paddle.

Rowing alone was a lot more difficult than I had expected. I hadn't realized how much work Clay was doing. My line was far from straight and I shuddered to think what the map looked like. My second lap was a little better. As I turned the boat around again, Clay tapped my shoulder with the transponder. I shook my head.

"Can I have another few laps? I almost got the hang of it."

"Yeah. Sure. Let me reset the map. This can be my second pass."

I ended up doing four more laps before trading Clay. By then, my arms were killing me. As I reset the map, I remembered we were kayaking in a pool. How much more difficult was it going to be next month when we were paddling against a river current?

Chapter 3

"Here we are." Professor Larkin pulled into the boat launch and cut the engine on his truck. Relieved, I took the last sip of my coffee and waited for someone to get out of the cab. I was sandwiched between my boss and Clay and I really needed to pee. Neither one of them seemed in a hurry to move.

Ultimately, Clay was faster. As soon as his seat was clear, I slid out, squeezing past him in the doorway and hightailing it to the portable restroom I saw at the edge of the lot. Normally, I avoided those things like the plague, but these were extenuating circumstances.

The car ride had been excruciating. The coffee had been a mistake, although it was well-appreciated when I was standing in the science faculty lot before dawn. After an hour on the highway, I realized I should have visited the restroom before climbing into the truck. After we pulled off the highway, we had hit enough bumps in the road that I was no longer certain my shorts were dry.

I returned to the truck in time to see Clay helping Professor Larkin remove the kayak from the bed. I watched them bring it to the edge of the waterline on the boat ramp, placing it sideways so it wouldn't drift into the water. I grabbed the raft and followed them. After I secured it to the back of the kayak, we made countless trips between the truck and the raft, loading our supplies. Professor Larkin would be checking in with us every three days to refill our food and water stores, but we still had a lot to carry. When the raft was full, Clay secured a tarp over the top and turned to Professor Larkin.

"All set."

"Great. Well, good luck. I will see you two in three days." He shook each of our hands before heading to the truck without even waiting for us to put the boats in the water.

"Hey. I got you something."

I turned back to Clay. "You did?"

Nodding, he handed me a small bag about the size of my wallet. I turned it over a few times. "Um, thanks?"

Clay gave a small laugh. "Open it."

I unzipped it, pulling out a long cord with a cuff on each end. I sent him a confused look. "I don't get it."

"It's a leash. Watch." He fastened one of the cuffs to my wrist before holding up the other end. For a moment, I thought he might attach it to himself, but he pointed to the kayak. "This end goes on your paddle. So you don't lose it in the river."

I was surprised by his thoughtfulness. Should I have gotten him some sort of camping supply? A solar power pack like the one I had borrowed from my father?

I couldn't quite meet his eye. "Thanks. You didn't have to do that."

He sent me a cocky smile. "Yeah, I did. We only have two paddles to last us all summer."

I glared at him. "Should we start this thing?"

We turned the kayak into the water, and I climbed in the front. After Clay passed me a paddle, he pushed the boat a little farther and climbed in behind me. Using our paddles, we pushed off the edge of the ramp into the Elver River.

The water was quiet at this hour. I could hear the occasional car passing on hidden roads and insects on the shore were buzzing and chirping. Nearby, a rooster was greeting the sunrise. But for the most part, all I heard was the sound of our paddles slapping against the water as we made our way to the opposite shore.

The river was about a quarter of a mile wide at this point and the current wasn't very strong. A few minutes after we set off, we were aligning the boat parallel to the shore. Clay's voice broke through the stillness of the morning.

"Dig your paddle into the ground to anchor us."

I watched as he demonstrated, then pushed my paddle into the soft dirt on the river side of the boat. As I held on, Clay hopped onto the shore. I sent him a curious look.

"Is this where we're storing the raft?"

"Nope." Clay tugged on the tether between the two boats, pulling the raft to shore. He reached under the tarp, removing a black reel of thin steel cable and a canvas bag nearly the length of the boat. After securing the tarp, he placed the bag on the shore and zipped it open. Inside were two of the orange poles the fire department usually used to mark hydrants for snow removal in the winter, each with a bright orange bullseye affixed to the top.

Clay pushed one of the stakes into the ground beside me before affixing the cable to a loop at the bottom. Slowly unraveling the reel, he tossed the bag and second stake into the kayak and returned to his seat. Without releasing my paddle, I turned to him.

"Um, what was that?"

Clay winked. "You'll see. We're going to hug the shore as best we can. The current isn't very strong, so you still need to paddle, but only a little."

I shrugged and turned back around, removing my paddle from the ground with a loud squelching sound. Pushing away from shore, I rowed lazily, letting our momentum carry us. Every few strokes, I would take a quick break, turning around to check on Clay. It didn't take long for him to run out of cable. Pushing my paddle into the shallow bottom, I guided us back to shore.

As I again anchored our boat with my paddle, Clay hopped out. He walked downstream until his cable was taut before pushing the pole into the ground and fastening the cable to the loop at the bottom. Retrieving the black bag from behind his seat, he pulled out a strange metal stick. It had a triangle on one end and a corkscrew on the other. I watched as Clay twisted the metal into the ground beside the marker, then yanked the triangle. He must have been pleased when it didn't move, because he untethered the supply boat from the kayak and clipped the carabiner into the triangle stake instead.

"There." He pulled the kayak slightly onto the shore with a satisfied grunt before unhooking the tracking boat from the back.

"Is this where we're making camp?"

Clay shook his head. "Nah. Just storing the boat here for an hour or so."

"Are you going to explain the orange bullseye thing?"

"In a few minutes. Here we go." He removed the chartplotter from the tracking boat, passing the transponder to me before clipping the boat to the kayak and climbing in.

"All set. Ready to start earning our paychecks?"

I shrugged. "I suppose."

"Great. Set up the map. Let me know when you're ready."

Even though the device was in some sort of plastic pouch, the touchscreen still worked and it took me less than a minute. "All set."

"Great. Grab your paddle."

I removed my anchor, placing it across the boat under my arms as I held the plotter in my lap. Clay pushed us away from the shore, turning the kayak upstream. As he paddled against the current, I watched the images on the chartplotter.

Clay waited until we were halfway back to the first bullseye before finally explaining their purpose. "The two markers are about a thousand feet apart, give or take a few inches. We're charting the space between them. When we're done, we'll move the markers downstream, along with the boat. Wherever we finish around sunset, that's where we'll camp for the night. Didn't Larkin explain all this to you during your interview?"

I shrugged. "It didn't really make much sense at the time."

Clay just shook his head, digging his paddle into the water and pushing us further along the river. When he reached the upstream marker, he turned the boat and scooted forward in his seat, letting the current push us downstream as he looked over my shoulder.

"How's the map coming?"

"Pretty good. We're overlapping some with the upstream data."

"That's a good thing. Makes the map more accurate."

"What happens when we reach the other shore?"

I glanced behind me to see Clay smile. "Then you get to row."

It took nearly half an hour to zigzag to the opposite shore. When Clay could no longer turn the boat without hitting land, I passed him the chartplotter and turned the boat.

Paddling in the river wasn't much more difficult than in the pool. The current was so mild, I could hardly feel it affecting the boat. Nevertheless, by the time we returned to the upstream marker, my arms were glad for a break.

I again held the boat steady while Clay retrieved the bullseye, then guided us downstream. By paddling lazily, we were able to coast slowly enough for Clay to spool the wire into a circle by his feet until we reached the supply boat. Leaving the bullseye and cable in the kayak, we both climbed out and pulled it onto the shore.

My legs were stiff from sitting with braced knees for so long. After retrieving my bag from the raft, I walked back and forth a few minutes to make sure my legs didn't fall asleep. Clay, meanwhile, tethered the supply boat to the back of the kayak before removing an energy bar from his bag.

"You should have a snack. We're not taking another break

until after twelve."

I shrugged. "I don't usually eat much in the morning. I'll be fine."

Clay didn't look convinced, but took another bite of his bar. I continued my pacing. When he was done, he shoved the wrapper in his bag and gestured to the boat. "Time to set sail."

I rolled my eyes as I climbed back into my seat. Once again, I made sure we didn't run aground while Clay unraveled the cable. When it was nearly gone, we pulled ashore and he secured the stake and raft.

The morning was extremely long. By noon, we had mapped nearly a mile of river and I was ready for a break. While I dragged the kayak ashore, Clay dug through the supply boat for the bag with our provisions.

Professor Larkin had provided us with three small coolers labeled with the days of the week. Last week, he had asked us each to email him with at least one week's worth of recipes for meals we could make on the camp store, complete with a list of ingredients we would need. Every three days, he would swap the coolers for us. While I was grateful we would not be eating dehydrated backpacking dinners, I was still hesitant about some of the meals I had selected.

Clay unearthed today's cooler from the supply boat and placed it between us on the ground. Inside, I found a plastic bottle that had once been a half gallon of juice but now contained a block of ice. Beside it was a six-pack of beer and several labeled plastic bags of food. I was surprised to see the beer, until I noticed the plastic sleeve containing a recipe printout. Beer was one of the ingredients.

On top of all of this sat the plastic bag we had gotten at the deli this morning. Inside, were two subs wrapped in paper. I removed them from the cooler, passing one to Clay.

"Thanks." He sat across from me as he unwrapped his lunch. "I have ham and cheese. What about you?"

I examined my own. "Same. You want my onions?"

"Sure, if you'll take my tomatoes."

I did my best to pick the onions off the sandwich and place them on Clay's wrapper. He put his tomatoes directly on my roll. I didn't mind.

We ate quickly and in silence. I wasn't sure what was going through Clay's head, but I was thinking about the rest of the day. Although I was enjoying myself, how long would it be before the newness wore off and the job became monotonous?

After lunch, we packed the cooler back into the raft and peed in the woods. I made sure to grab my water from my bag before returning to the kayak. Clay clipped the supply boat to the back and took his seat. As I rowed, he slowly unwound the chain until we could secure the bullseye marker downstream.

We saw more life on the river as the day progressed. Even though it was a Monday, the beautiful weather brought other boaters to the area, mostly kayaks, although there was the occasional motorboat. Each time one passed, Clay and I had to fight against its wake to keep the kayak straight. A few people sent curious looks at the tracking boat, but for most part, they just waved as they passed.

I took the first paddling shift after lunch. As we made our way back to the upstream marker, Clay tried to start a conversation.

"You seem to be getting the hang of this. Maybe you should join the crew team next year."

I scoffed. "Yeah, right. I'll just apply to grad school while I'm rowing."

"Any idea what you're going to study?"

I shrugged. "No. I was hoping this internship might make me want to study marine biology or ecology. But, it feels more like I'm on this boating adventure than working."

I glanced back in time to see Clay smile. "Yeah. I get that. I'm focusing on ecology myself. I liked the idea of spending so much time with nature. I'm not going to lie, though." He held up the chartplotter. "Part of me is hoping this little doohickey helps us find Elver."

A motorboat passed, forcing me to focus on paddling against the wake. The boat was too loud for me to respond anyway. But, as my blade dug through the water, I couldn't help but wonder what I would see when we uploaded our data that evening.

We wouldn't really find any evidence of a river monster, would we?

Chapter 4

After a long day of paddling, I was looking forward to a hot shower and a warm bed. Unfortunately, I would not have either for nearly two months. As the sun fell behind the trees, Clay and I brought the boat ashore to set up our camp.

I could see a house through the thin trees, but I knew we had permission to camp on the immediate shore. While Clay secured the boats to the triangle anchor, I pulled a duffel bag from the raft and scouted the area.

We only had a small clearing, but there was just enough space for a tent. I removed it from the bag, aligning it so the door was facing the water. Pulling on the handle in the center, the tent was ready in less than a minute. With a smile of satisfaction, I returned to the raft.

"So, how are we supposed to cook the hot dogs? Campfire?"

Clay shook his head. "No. We're not allowed to make fires unless we're at an actual campground." He reached into the raft, removing a red bag with two green cylinders in pockets on the sides. "We've got a stove."

While he set up the stove between the boat and the water, I brought our packs and bedrolls to the tent. After growing lightheaded inflating my air mattress, I unrolled my sleeping bag and set up my bed. I considered helping Clay with his, but it felt like an invasion of his privacy.

Clay was sitting by the stove with a beer in his hand. In front of him lay several of the plastic bags. I watched as he poured his beer into a bag with white powder. He pulled a white chunk out of one bag, placed it in the bag with the beer, then returned it to the first bag. After doing this with several chunks, he zipped the bag closed and shook it.

A skillet sat over the fire on the stove. Clay poured a drop of his beer into it. Smiling at the hiss, he threw two of the coated chunks in it. I sat beside him.

"What's for supper?"

Clay smiled at me. "There's some hummus and carrot sticks in the cooler. Grab those, leave everything else."

I pointed to the stove. "That's not hummus."

"Nope. This is a recipe I wanted to try. Grab the mess kits from the tub."

A plastic container about the size of a dish strainer was sitting beside him. Mixed with some dried foodstuffs, I found a kettle, a small pot, and two mesh totes. After replacing the lid on the tub, I emptied the two bags and set the tub like a table. We each had a plate, cup, and utensils. By the time I retrieved the food from the cooler, Clay had placed a fried chunk on each of our plates and thrown two more into the skillet.

It smelled delicious, but I didn't want to be rude. I returned to the cooler. "Am I allowed a beer? Or is it just for cooking?"

"Oh, by all means. Grab me one, too. I didn't really drink this one. It mostly went into the batter."

After placing the second chunks on our plates, Clay turned off the stove and dumped his water bottle into the skillet before holding his beer out toward me.

"Cheers."

I clinked my can to his. "Cheers. So, what is this?"

"Beer-battered halibut."

"Smells delicious."

I took a bite. It tasted even better than it smelled. I eagerly ate it before it grew cold.

After a few moments, I asked, "So, how long until we get to the lake?"

"Why? Anxious to meet Elver?"

"It's not real, you know."

"Then why do people go missing every year?"

"Maybe they go kayaking without life jackets."

Clay shook his head, lowering his voice as if telling a ghost story. "Legend has it that Elver can sense who believes in him. Whenever an unbeliever crosses the center of the lake, BAM!" Clay clapped his hands together, making me jump. "He takes them as proof."

"What good does that do? If they die, they can't really become a believer.”

“They can haunt the lake, warning others about Elver.”

I shook my head. “Yeah. Keep telling yourself that.”

Clay pointed to me with his beer. “You’ll see. We’ll reach the lake within a week and then you’ll believe.”

I just rolled my eyes and dipped a carrot in the hummus.

After supper, we used the plastic tub to wash the dishes, then finished our beers as we stared at the stars. One of the neighbors was having a party, sending bright lights and loud music across the water. Clay and I compared our classes until our drinks were gone. After returning all the trash to the cooler and stowing all the cooking supplies in the tub, we climbed into our sleeping bags.

Despite the music and the early hour, I was exhausted. I had been up before dawn and rowed for hours. Resting my head on my bag, I quickly fell asleep.

I was alone in the tent when I woke. Clay was taking a quick swim in the river. After venturing in the opposite direction to pee in the woods, I went to see what I could do about breakfast.

In the cooler was a plastic container with half a dozen eggs. There was also a bag of cheese and another with fresh spinach. After setting up the stove, I found oil in the big tub and heated it in the skillet. I used the pan to scramble the eggs with some cheese while the spinach was cooking. Clay came out of the water as I poured the mixture into the pan.

“Mmm. What’s for breakfast?”

“Scrambled eggs.”

“Smells great. Where’s the coffee?”

My eyes widened. “There’s coffee?”

Clay shook his damp head as he made his way toward the tent. “Check the tub.”

Sure enough, there was a container of instant coffee. Since the ice in the cooler had melted, I poured some of the water into the kettle. As soon as the eggs were done, I put the kettle on the stove.

Clay returned in clean clothes and we ate the eggs while they were warm. When our plates were empty, he washed dishes and I stole a few minutes to give myself a quick sponge bath in the tent before changing into clean clothes. After packing up my bedding, I collapsed the tent and stowed everything in the raft.

Our second day went much like the first. Since the river narrowed slightly, we were able to do fewer laps each time we set up the markers. Paddling was becoming easier as well. Although it was still difficult, I found myself struggling less when each boat passed.

However, it was still monotonous. Despite the fact that I was sharing a boat, I was beginning to feel lonely. After I rowed a second time, I tried to start a conversation, turning slightly so I could see Clay.

"My roommate thought I was crazy for taking a summer job that meant I wouldn't be able to use my phone. It feels weird not being able to check my feed every hour."

Clay laughed. "My girlfriend felt the same way. Though, I think she was more upset I couldn't text her every five minutes."

"I . . . didn't think you had a girlfriend."

"I don't. We broke up when I told her I was taking this job."

"That's . . . messed up."

Clay shrugged. "Yeah, well, so was our relationship. She was one of those obsessive types. Always texting me. Freaking out if I took more than a minute to respond. Always accusing me of flirting with other girls."

"Were you?"

Clay sent me a mischievous smile. "Never on purpose. How about you?"

"Me what?"

"You seeing anyone?"

"No." Since I could hear the definitiveness in my voice, I was pretty sure Clay had as well.

He smirked. "Ooh. That *no* sounded like there was a story behind it."

I sighed. "I was seeing this guy most of last semester. We would go out to eat, watch movies together. Had a great time. Til the night his girlfriend walked in on us."

Clay winced. "Ouch."

I shrugged. "Technically, we never said we weren't seeing other people."

Clay shook his head as he turned the boat. "Yeah, I've never really understood that. Why would anyone want the hassle of seeing more than one person at once? If I like someone, I want to give her all my attention. Why would I try to split it between two women?"

I felt the same way, but this conversation was growing too intense for me. Thankfully, a passing motorboat made talking difficult.

Three miles later, we set up our camp for the evening. While Clay made supper, I again erected the tents. But, instead of helping him make whatever he was preparing, I put on my bathing suit and grabbed the biodegradable soap we used on my family camping trips.

I felt like a medieval peasant washing my clothes at the edge of the water. Even if we ever reached a real campground, I doubted they would have laundry facilities. I was going to have to do this all summer.

At least I wasn't washing my underwear. It would have been very embarrassing to have my bras and panties drying on the side of the kayak. I had only been wearing bathing suits and shorts for the past few days.

After laying my clothes on the boat, I waded into the river. I tried not to think about what might be swimming with me as I used the soap to wash my hair and scrub my body.

Refreshed, I changed into a clean outfit and joined Clay as he was placing the meal on our plates. I sat across from him, inhaling deeply.

"Smells fantastic. What is it?"

"Chicken fajitas." He gestured to the flour tortillas and take-out size containers of sour cream. "Eat up."

I spread a little sour cream on a tortilla and spooned some chicken on top. The cheese had been mixed in with the peppers and onions, making everything melty. Although it could have benefited from some hot sauce, the meal was pretty good.

Our days blended together, one day melting into the next. The skies remained clear and the temperature was not oppressive. I couldn't imagine a better summer job.

Clay and I spent our time on the water talking about our best and worst classes, his being on the crew team, and even the past relationships that still haunted us. By the end of the week, he had become a good friend and I was enjoying spending my days with him.

Wednesday afternoon, we spotted a campground on the opposite shore. It was an unexpected surprise. I hadn't thought we would reach one before getting to the lake.

After setting up the orange targets, we rowed directly to one of the empty river sites. While Clay held the paddle as an anchor, I set up a new map, placing the transponder on my seat before climbing out of the boat.

"You sure you can do this alone?"

Clay nodded. "I'll be fine. This part is so narrow, I'll probably be done before you."

I shook my head, untethering the supply boat and dragging it ashore. "Yeah, I don't think so."

"Is that a dare?" He winked. "Loser makes supper?"

"You're on."

"Then . . . Go!"

He pushed away from the shore, turning the boat to paddle upstream. Smiling to myself, I unearthed my pack from the raft and set out along the trail.

I followed the wooded path for nearly ten minutes before reaching the camp office. The small log cabin contained a single person sitting behind the counter. She sent me a warm smile as I entered.

"Hi. How can I help you?"

"Hi. My coworker and I are rowing downstream this summer. We were wondering if we could have a river site for the night. Here."

I passed her the note Larkin had written explaining our project. She glanced at it quickly before turning to her computer.

"How long will you be staying?"

"Just the night. Oh, and I need firewood."

The keys clacked for a moment before she turned back to me. "All four sites are available. Did you have a particular one in mind?"

"Well, we pulled our boat ashore at site four, but we can move it."

She shook her head. "Four works fine." She entered some information into the computer, occasionally referring to Larkin's letter before returning it to me.

"You are all set. I just need a card."

I took out the debit card Larkin had given me for this type of expense. The woman returned it with a map of the campground and a bundle of firewood.

"All set."

"Thanks."

As I returned to the campsite, I turned on my phone. Although I had been charging it with my father's solar charger, I had decided to leave it off when I wasn't using it. Solar panels only worked on sunny days, and there had been a lot of clouds this week.

When the phone booted, I was pleased to see I had reception. I sent my parents and roommate quick texts to let them know I was still alive before stopping at the bathhouse on my way back to the campsite.

It was nice to use a toilet again, but what I really wanted was a warm shower. I hadn't expected to see running water until the end of the summer. I was even more thrilled that the showers weren't coin-operated.

I brought all my clothes with me into the shower, washing everything I wasn't planning on wearing that night. Though the pressure was low and the water only lukewarm, by the time I dressed, I felt nearly human again.

Bundling my wet clothes in my towel, I shouldered my pack and grabbed my phone and firewood. Clay was pulling the kayak ashore.

"Ha. I got here first. You're cooking."

I shook my head. "I finished a while ago. I was taking a shower and doing laundry."

"That sounds like a great idea. I'll do that while you cook."

Clay didn't wait for me to respond. He grabbed his pack from the raft and disappeared along the trail. After double checking that the boats were secure, I threw a few logs in the fire pit along with some twigs and leaves, igniting them with the stick lighter we used on the stove.

When the tinder caught, I dragged the picnic table close to the fire, laying my wet clothes along the bench. Then, I set up the camp stove and found the last cooler. I was surprised the food was still cold after three days, although the bottle of ice was nearly melted.

Following the recipe in the cooler, I threw some rice and beans in a pot with a bag of spices and other assorted ingredients. While that simmered, I set up the tent and beds. Clay returned just as I was turning off the stove.

"I checked in with Larkin," he informed me as he laid his wet things on the table. "He said we're close to the lake. He wants us to leave the raft here in the morning. He'll come pick it up and bring it to the campground on the lake for us."

It was nice to relax by the fire, especially knowing we would be doing it again the next night.

Would the entire summer be this pleasant?

Chapter 5

Thursday morning started off much like every other. As Clay made breakfast, I broke camp. We stowed the remaining firewood in the raft and placed our lunches in a small bag in the kayak.

It felt weird to leave the supply boat behind. Clay had left the markers on the opposite shore. We moved the upper one downstream and began our day.

During lunch, Clay examined a laminated map Larkin had given him and decided the river had narrowed so much, we could get the data in a single lap. We would not need the markers until we reached the lake. And without doing multiple laps, we would probably reach the campground by sunset.

Knowing we were so close to the lake made us a little sloppy. While Clay rowed, I turned slightly so I could see him as we discussed which professor was the worst in the department. After I explained the horror of my first semester of biology, he shook his head.

"I'll give you that she's not the best Bio 101 professor. But, her environmental health and safety class is really good. No. Hemingway for genetics. That's—" He swore.

"I liked that class."

A look of panic passed over his face. "Hold on!"

I turned around in time to see the water growing rough. We had wedged the orange markers in the pocket on the side of the boat meant for storing the paddles. I wedged the transponder in the pocket on my opposite end and picked up my paddle.

I had just dipped it in the water when I realized we were heading toward a rock. I rowed on the right side of the boat until we were out of danger.

Before I could relax, I had to frantically paddle on the opposite side to avoid another rock. I shouted to Clay above the rushing water.

"What do we do?"

"Look straight ahead. See how the water makes an arrow?"

Water sprayed in my eyes, but I tried to squint past it. In between the white crests, the water formed a dark V shape, pointing toward the eastern shore.

"I see it."

"Okay. Pretend this is a video game. You want to go over the arrows like they're power boosters."

I wanted to smile, but I was too scared. My heart was racing as I tried to angle the boat. As soon as we went over the arrow, I immediately scanned for the next one. I didn't see it until Clay started turning the boat toward the western shore.

I paddled frantically toward it, splashing water all over myself.

"Calm down!" Clay yelled from behind me. "Deep, purposeful strokes."

I wasn't sure how he could remain so calm. I was certain we were going to die. But, I did as he said, digging my blade further into the water as I angled the boat toward the next arrow.

Finally, the river widened and the water slowed down. Clay pointed toward the shore with his paddle.

"Pull alongside there."

My ears were ringing from the rushing water and my heart was in overdrive. But it wasn't until we were anchoring that I realized I had a death grip on my paddle.

Clay sent me a concerned look as he dug his paddle into the muddy bottom. "You okay?"

I let out a shaky breath. "Maybe? Did you know those were there?"

Clay shook his head. "No, but I'm kicking myself for not expecting it."

"Well, at least it's over." When Clay grimaced, my eyes grew wide. "You mean there are more?"

"There might be. But, I was still thinking about these. Did we get the data, or do we need a second run? If we go too fast, the transponder doesn't work well."

I looked past him toward the little boat bobbing behind us. "Did the tracker break?"

Clay pulled on the string until the boat was beside him, then examined it carefully. "Looks okay. Did we get data the whole time?"

I pulled the tablet from its pocket and passed it to Clay. I would let him make the decision. He shook his head back and forth as he scrolled through the data on the screen. I still had no idea what most of it meant, but he seemed able to read it.

"I think it will be okay."

I let out a breath I didn't realize I had been holding. "So, we can continue downriver?"

Clay smiled at me. "So, we can continue downriver."

Clay and I paddled in silence as we turned a corner. I wasn't sure about him, but I was thinking about our harrowing brush with death. Well, maybe it hadn't been that bad, but it was one of the scariest things in my life.

Until we reached the next set.

These rapids were even stronger. The front of the boat dipped underwater. I leaned backwards to help shift my weight. Clay turned the boat into the V.

But we missed and ended up cresting over the wave. We landed hard and I bounced in my seat. For the first time that week, I wished I had a seat belt.

I pushed on my pedals, pressing my knees against the inner edge of the boat as hard as I could. I was moving my paddle from one side of the kayak to the other, but I wasn't sure the blade was even making contact with the water.

I couldn't think. My heart was racing. Water was spraying in my face making it difficult to see. I could hear Clay shouting to me, but I had no idea what he was saying.

One more arrow, I told myself. *One more arrow and we'll be out of this.*

I scanned the area for the next V. When I found it, I angled the kayak straight toward it. I didn't dare glance at Clay, but he and I must have been in sync. The boat was moving exactly the way I wanted it to.

As soon as the front of the boat went over the arrow, I searched for the next one. I continued, repeating "one more arrow" to myself until we were clear of the rapids.

With a huge sigh of relief, I flopped back in my seat, closing my eyes as I let my head fall backwards. Panting, I let the boat drift while I waited for my heart to stop racing.

"We did it."

When Clay didn't respond, I opened my eyes. His upside-down seat was empty. I quickly sat up and turned around.

Clay was not in the boat.

"Clay?"

I looked everywhere. He wasn't floating nearby. I couldn't see him in the rapids.

I quickly rowed to the edge of the river, turning the kayak before anchoring myself with my paddle. I could feel my heart pounding in my chest, and I wasn't sure if it was exertion or panic.

I scanned the water back and forth for a long time. Clay was nowhere to be seen. I called his name. The only reply was the roar of the rapids.

We had never discussed what to do in this situation. I had always assumed I would be the one falling out of the boat and when I did so, Clay would help me back in. But now he was missing.

After a few minutes, I saw something floating down the rapids. When it got stuck on a rock, I realized it was a paddle. Clay's paddle. The one that had been tethered to him.

Relief flooded through me. He was okay.

The rock was off to the side, out of the way of the strongest part of the current. With great difficulty, I managed to bring the kayak alongside it. With greater difficulty, I was able to grab the paddle without falling out of the boat.

The leash was still on the paddle. The cuff was open, as if Clay had removed it on purpose. I couldn't understand why.

I had no idea what I should do. Was Clay floating unconscious near one of the rocks? Was he sitting by the side of the river waiting for me to rescue him? Was he even above water?

I needed advice. My first instinct was that Clay would know what to do. Since I couldn't ask him, I decided to try Larkin. Except, I didn't have my phone. It was in my pack, in the raft.

I would have to find the campground. I hated the idea of abandoning Clay, but I didn't have any other choice. I turned the kayak around and continued downstream.

The river turned and around the bend, I could see the lake. I had no idea where to find the campground. As the water widened, I tried to stay in the middle, looking in both directions as I paddled. But all I saw were trees and the occasional dock. Nothing to indicate the campground. When the sun began to disappear behind the trees, seeing became even more difficult. Without realizing it, I was hugging the western shore.

The lake was at least three times larger than the widest part of the river. But, the campground was nowhere to be found. Eventually, I reached the southern end. I could clearly see the passage to continue downriver. Skimming across it, I paddled to the opposite side of the lake and headed upstream.

The campground was in the middle of the shore. Part of the lake was marked by buoys to denote a swimming hole. As I paddled around it, I saw campfires in the distance.

After passing a boat launch ramp, I began to see fires dotting the shore. I looked for the supply raft, assuming Larkin would do his best to get us a riverfront site. But, as the light faded, it became difficult to see anything.

More than once I considered turning around to take the boat out at the launch. I could go to the camp office, ask about my site. Maybe find someone to help me carry the boat there.

I had just decided that was the best plan when I saw the raft. The tent was set up behind a blazing fire. The man sitting beside it waved as I approached. He rose to assist me as I brought the kayak ashore.

I stared at him, opening and closing my mouth a few times before I could finally make words.

"But . . . How?"

Clay smiled, steadying the boat so I could climb out. "It's a long story that requires a beer or two."

I helped him pull the boat onto the grass. "But, you're okay?"

"I'm okay."

Without thinking, I threw my arms around him. "I was so worried. I didn't know what to do."

He pushed me away gently. "*El Cafecito*, you're shaking. Come warm up by the fire."

I tossed my life jacket into the kayak, but I wasn't shaking from cold. It was relief.

Clay passed me a beer as I sat beside him, our backs against the edge of the picnic table. I took a long gulp, downing half the bottle. Clay laughed.

"Easy, killer."

"I was so scared. I had no idea what to do."

Clay put an arm around me. "Hey. Everything's okay now. Why don't you go put on dry clothes?"

I nodded. "That's a good idea. But, what happened to you?"

Clay remained by the fire as I crawled into the tent. But, I could still hear his response.

"You first. Did you fall out, too? I expected you here a long time ago."

As I changed, I told him about searching for him and finding his paddle. When I returned to the fire, I laid my wet clothes beside his on the picnic table while explaining the difficulty I had finding the campsite.

Clay passed me a bowl of chili as I plopped beside him. I took a slow bite with my eyes closed.

"This is perfect. Just what I needed."

Clay smiled. "Good."

"So, what happened to you? How did you get *here*?"

"When I fell out, I tried calling to you. I guess you didn't hear me. The current took me and my paddle. I tried swimming, but the current was too strong. It was easier to float."

"But, your paddle came out of the rapids. You didn't."

Clay shook his head. "I was getting tangled in the tether, so I took off the cuff. Made it much easier to swim. I got out of the rapids and headed to shore. Walked inland and just past the trees this guy was pushing his kid on the swings. The kid screamed. Thought I was the lake monster."

"You're not that scary looking."

Clay bumped his shoulder against mine as he took a sip of his beer. "Well, the kid thought so. I told them what happened and told him I expected you at the campsite. The guy drove me here and the office told me which site was ours."

"Did you call Larkin? Tell him what happened?"

"Yeah." A flash of anger crossed Clay's face.

I sent him a curious look. "Are you in trouble?"

Clay shook his head. "Larkin didn't care I got thrown from the boat. Like, he couldn't care less. All he cared about was his precious experiment. Was the boat okay? The tracker."

I called Larkin a very insulting name that made Clay smile. He put an arm around me. "Yeah, he is. But, you were worried about me." As I turned to face him, he tucked a stray hair behind my ear.

My voice came out as a whisper. "Yeah. I was."

He leaned a little closer. "I was worried about you, too."

I could feel his warm breath on my face. Since I didn't know what to say, I inched forward until our lips met.

The campfire wasn't the only thing warding off my chill.

Chapter 6

I awoke to the sound of rain pounding the tent. But, the noise wasn't as disorienting as the sleeping arrangements. Clay's chest was my pillow, his arm around my shoulders. His unzipped sleeping bag was beneath us while mine covered us like a blanket.

A flash of lightning illuminated the tent, bright enough to see Clay in only his boxers. That was more than I was wearing. The rumble of thunder caused Clay to stir, pulling me closer.

"Mmm. What time is it?"

"I don't know."

Another flash was immediately followed by thunder. The storm was on top of us. Clay pulled me closer.

"We're not going to be able to work today."

I traced my finger along his chest. "You mean we're stuck here all day? What are we going to do?"

"Oh, I have a few ideas." His lips met mine as his hands made their way down my body.

With no reason to do otherwise, Clay and I spent our morning in the tent. When the lightning stopped, Clay pulled on a pair of shorts to make his way to the bathhouse. I threw on a shirt and peed in the woods. The bathhouse was too far away in the rain.

Turning on the cook stove would have drenched me, so I decided I would be fine with granola for breakfast. I wasn't too concerned about eating in the tent, since it was easy enough to shake out any crumbs when the rain passed. I just wished I had coffee.

Clay took a while in the bathroom. Long enough for me to start wondering whether sleeping with him had been a mistake. We had both just had bad breakups and I doubted either of us were ready for a relationship. So, this was more likely a one-night stand.

This was new territory for me. I had always avoided one-nighters because I never wanted the uncomfortable feeling of seeing the guy in one of my classes, or even just on the path, and not knowing what to say.

How was I supposed to spend the rest of the summer working with Clay? Especially on days like today when we were stuck inside a tent?

I heard a commotion above the din of the rain and peeked my head outside the tent flap. Clay was leafing through the supplies on the raft. A moment later, he secured the tarp and ran back to the tent, his arms full.

"What are you doing?" I asked as I zipped the flap behind him. I pointed to the camp stove. "You're not seriously thinking of lighting that in here."

He shook his head, running his hands through my hair. "That's for later. Right now . . ."

When his lips met mine, there was no heat, no urgency. It was passionate, but in a gentle way.

The sky had brightened slightly when I rolled away from Clay. He reached over to stroke my hair. "I could do this all day."

I smiled. "I would agree, but I think I'm going to need to eat something soon."

As if to emphasize my point, my stomach grumbled loudly. Clay kissed it before sitting up. "I'll make breakfast."

"I'm okay with just granola."

"Well, I'm not."

Clay threw on his boxers before unzipping the tent flap. Between it and the rain fly, there was a small space where we normally kept our shoes. After throwing a towel on the tent floor, Clay moved the muddy footwear inside and set the camp stove in their place. I crawled beside him.

"That can't be safe."

He smiled at me. "I strongly recommend you put on a shirt

because otherwise, you might distract me and the tent will go up in flames."

To prove his point, he kissed me. I wanted to pull him back onto the bed, but my growling stomach killed the mood. Giggling, I crawled to my bag to retrieve a tank top.

"So, um, can we talk about, well, this?"

Clay let out an exasperated huff. "I've done this before. It's really not a big deal."

All of my concerns from earlier rushed back to me. I let out a shaky breath. "So, when the rain stops and we go back to work tomorrow?"

"I'll make dinner out on the picnic table."

I sent him a confused look. "Huh?"

He turned to me, his expression nearly as baffled as I felt. "I'm only doing this cause of the rain. It's not like I'm going to do this every meal. And, frankly, I would never expect you to do this."

I shook my head. "I wasn't talking about the stove. I was talking about—" I couldn't say it out loud. I gestured weakly toward our sleeping bags.

With a smirk, Clay crawled beside me. He put an arm around my waist, running his other hand through my hair as he pulled me close.

"I have liked you since I met you that night in Elver Ale. Then I saw you on the pool deck and I found out I would be working with you all summer. I almost asked you out that night. But, I figured I'd wait to see how you felt."

My response was barely a whisper. "And what did you decide?"

"Oh, you pretended like you didn't care about me. But, last night, you made a mistake."

"Yeah? What was that?"

His lips brushed against mine and yet I could barely hear his whisper over the rain. "You hugged me when you saw me."

His kiss was slow and sweet, containing none of the urgency it had last night. I pulled him closer, leading him back toward the beds. Before we reached the ground, the tea kettle whistled.

Clay sat back with a smile. "Breakfast is ready."

I ran my hands through his messy hair. "I just hear water. What could you have possibly made?"

"Oatmeal. And coffee."

I brought my face close to his. "I don't smell any coffee."

"Well, I'll just have to fix that, won't I?"

He crawled to the cooking bin, removing the mess kits. I pulled out mugs while he dug through the box to retrieve the instant coffee and some oatmeal in disposable bowls. We made our breakfasts in silence, then sat on opposite ends of the tent while we ate.

I gestured toward the flap with my spoon. "So, I'm assuming this storm is going to last most of the day?"

A roll of thunder responded before Clay could. He nodded. "Yeah. Probably."

"So, any ideas about what we should do while we're waiting it out?"

He sent me a lascivious look. "Oh, I have lots of ideas. But, I was thinking we set up my phone as a mobile hot spot and upload all the data we collected this week."

That was not the response I had been expecting and I had no idea how to answer. "Um, sure?"

He leaned across the tent until our faces were only inches apart. "Don't worry. There will be plenty of time for other things. We have all day." He kissed me before returning to his oatmeal.

It didn't take long to upload the data to the chartplotting server, but we wouldn't be able to see the results for a few days. By then, we would be mapping the lake. While we waited for the transponder to finish sending the information, Clay pulled out his laminated map of the lake, pointing to the campground.

"We're here. I suggest tomorrow, we start here." He moved his finger to the northernmost part of the lake. "Then we can—"

I shook my head. "I think we should start here." I pointed to where the river entered the lake. "It will be much easier to find. If we go your way, we may have trouble figuring out where the top-most part is."

"Works for me. Who's calling?"

He glanced at the readout on his ringing phone. Swearing, he showed me the display.

Larkin.

I held out my hand. "Want me to talk to him?"

"I'll put it on speaker. Hi, Professor Larkin."

"Clay? What are you doing? I got a message that you are uploading the maps to the server."

Clay raised his eyebrows at me. "Aren't we supposed to?"

"Yes. At night. During the day, you're supposed to be mapping the lake."

Clay waited until the thunder passed before responding. "It's too dangerous to be out in a boat today."

"You're going to let a little rain stop you?"

I glared at the phone. "It's not—"

Clay put up a hand, shaking his head as he interrupted me. "It's not the rain. We were prepared to go out in the rain today. But, I can't go on the lake when there's lightning. It's not safe. And it could ruin the tracking device."

Larkin let out an exasperated sigh. "Fine. But, you are not going to be paid for days you don't work."

I rolled my eyes and Clay made a rude hand gesture as Larkin ended the call. He then proceeded to call our boss a long string of insulting, albeit creative, names.

Giggling, I moved closer to Clay. "That was a good idea. Threatening the safety of the tracker."

"It's all he cares about. He couldn't care less if one of us got hurt out there."

I ran my hand along his leg. "That's okay. We'll look out for each other."

Clay nodded, kissing me gently. Before it could turn into something more, I sat back and grabbed my phone. "I just want to make sure this storm really will last all day."

The flash of lighting and peal of thunder should have been enough to convince me. But, I searched my weather app nonetheless, snuggled against Clay.

"Yeah, thunderstorms through the night." I sent him a mischievous smile. "Guess we're going to have to find ways to amuse ourselves inside today."

He passed me his phone. "Maybe by researching more on this?"

The screen showed an article from one of the local papers. I could see instantly why the headline had grabbed Clay's attention.

Elver Attacks: Man Missing

According to the article, a man went missing Saturday afternoon after fishing in Elver Lake. His body was discovered the following morning when it washed up downriver. I rolled my eyes as I returned the phone to Clay.

"You know, they make life jackets for a reason. The guy probably capsized and well, drowned."

"So, you don't believe in the monster?"

I shook my head. "Do you?"

Clay frowned. "I'm not saying that it does exist. I'm just not going to say that it's not possible."

I turned to face him. "Is this one of those deep-set beliefs that is going to make things difficult between us?"

He pulled me closer. "It's going to take a lot more than a lake monster to get between us."

"So, is this more than a one-night thing?"

Clay ran his fingers through his hair. "I may have texted my roommate while I was in the bathhouse. And, I may have mentioned to him that I have a new girlfriend."

I smirked. "Oh, good. Then I can send my roommate that same text."

"Really? You have a new girlfriend, too?"

Among the supplies in his bag, Clay had packed a deck of cards. We spent our afternoon teaching each other new games. Around sunset, the storm calmed long enough to boil a pot of water for supper. The kettle had just started whistling when the rain restarted. Clay packed up the stove while I poured the water into our bowls. Storing the kettle under the rain flap, I followed Clay into the tent just as the skies opened.

While the rain made a thunderous noise, we ate our macaroni and cheese and searched for more news about the missing man. Though most of the local papers were quick to blame the lake monster, the news stations and more regional papers had other theories.

"I still say it's possible he swam out too far and drowned." I glanced at Clay to gauge his opinion.

"I'm not discounting that. But, will you admit that it is also possible that *something* lives under the water and pulled him under."

"Like a water dragon?" I turned my phone, showing Clay the image in most of the articles. It was nearly identical to the cartoon creature posted on Larkin's bulletin board.

Clay smirked. "No. I doubt there's a water dragon. I was thinking like an eel. Maybe an alligator."

I raised my eyebrows. "Don't you think people would know if there's an alligator? Besides, the river's what? Thirty, forty feet deep? The lake probably isn't much deeper. I thought alligators liked shallower water."

Clay searched his phone a moment. "The river's around 100 feet deep, although it was much shallower at the rapids yesterday. But, gators prefer . . . it doesn't say and I guess it's probably too cold for an alligator. But, maybe it's an eel. Or an octopus!"

I rolled my eyes. "Seriously? An octopus? This far upriver?"

Clay shrugged. "It could happen. Look! This is an article about sightings of monsters in this river. They date back to colonial days."

I moved closer to him, reading the article over his shoulder before looking at him.

"Fine. I will admit that there is a possibility that an octopus or eel might live in the lake."

Clay tossed the phone aside, sending me a mischievous smile as he threw his arms around me. "That's all I wanted to hear."

Chapter 7

The sun was peeking over the horizon and birds were already singing in the trees when Clay's alarm woke us Saturday morning. He silenced it before rolling over and kissing me.

"Morning." He tucked a hair behind my ear.

I smiled. "Morning."

"I *really* don't want to go to work today."

I gave him a quick kiss. "Me neither. But, look at it this way. The sooner we get to work, the sooner we can take a lunch break. Here at the tent." I traced a finger down his bare chest.

"I like that idea."

His kiss was interrupted by his alarm. Clay swore. "I thought I turned that thing off."

I sat up. "You probably just hit snooze. Hey, look on the bright side. We don't have to pack up the camp this morning. And, since it's not raining, I'm thinking eggs for breakfast."

I threw on a shirt and made my way outside. Clay emerged from the tent a moment later in a pair of shorts, his pack over one shoulder. He kissed my cheek.

"I'm going to take a shower and then I'll help with breakfast."

"I'll probably be finished by the time you get back."

"Is that a dare?" Clay's eyes sparkled. "Loser cleans dishes?"

I shook my head. "You're cleaning dishes no matter what."

"In that case ... Go!" He jogged toward the bathhouse. Smiling, I pulled the eggs from the cooler.

Clay returned as I was placing the breakfast on the plates. After pouring steaming water into the instant coffee, I sat beside him. He smelled like real soap, not the camp stuff I had been using. I inhaled deeply.

He raised his eyebrows. "You okay?"

I quickly picked up my coffee. "Yeah. I'm fine. Breakfast just smells so good."

I could tell by his smirk he didn't believe me, but he said nothing. When I was done eating, I left him to the dishes and dug through the tent for my pack. I contemplated borrowing Clay's body wash—without telling him, of course—but decided our relationship was too new for that step. I would steal it next week instead.

I charged my phone while I showered and brushed my teeth and hair. I wished I could leave it there all day, but I didn't want anyone to take it. Turning it off to save the battery, I headed back to the campsite.

Clay had already cleared breakfast and was angling the kayak for us to return it to the water. He held out my life jacket as I approached.

"Ready to go?"

"Let's do it."

As I grabbed my jacket, he pulled it close to him, causing me to stumble into his arms. He stole a quick kiss before releasing it.

"That's so neither of us falls out today."

"You just don't want to get eaten by the giant octopus."

Clay swore. "Why'd you have to go put that in my head?"

"Because it's not real. Come on. Let's go. I want to try to get four markers done before lunch."

We put the kayak in the water, and I held it steady as Clay climbed aboard. While I waited for him to attach his paddle leash to his wrist, I glanced at the lake. At this hour, it was completely still.

"All set."

I turned my attention back to Clay. Wordlessly, he pointed toward the tracker boat. Rolling my eyes, I retrieved it, passing him the transponder before attaching the clip to the kayak. After handing him the orange markers, I climbed into the boat. Just before I placed my paddle in the water, I thought I saw something break the glassy surface.

I pointed. "Did you see that?"

"See what?"

"Nothing."

Clay leaned forward, kissing the top of my head. "Starting to believe in Elver?"

"No. I was just wondering what kind of fish jumps out of the water."

Clay pushed us away from shore. "Sure you were."

We paddled to the mouth of the lake, placing the markers on the eastern shore and moving northward into a small cove. Clay had just secured the upstream bullseye when a man came charging toward us, shaking his fist in the air. He was built like a linebacker and, judging by his temper, had yet to have his morning coffee. When he bellowed, his voice was gruff and unfriendly.

"What do you kids think you're doing?"

I was scared and angry at the same time, but Clay seemed to maintain his composure. "We're conducting a bathymetric survey of the area. These stakes are to monitor our progress. We'll remove them in an hour or so."

The man glowered at us. "Doesn't look like much of a survey. Looks like two kids playing in a kayak."

I held up the transponder. "This device scans the bottom of the lake to help us determine how deep it is."

"How does it tell the difference between the bottom of the lake and the fish?"

Clay smiled. "There's this little guy taking pictures inside the machine. He looks at them. If it's a fish, he tosses the picture away. If it's the floor, he makes a note on his map. We only feed him if he gives us accurate maps."

I was trying not to laugh, but the man was less than amused. His glare clearly indicated he wanted to hurt Clay. "One hour. You have one hour to get that thing off my property, or I call the cops. You hear me?"

"We'll go as quickly as we can, sir." Clay pushed away from the shore, turning the boat to the downstream marker.

The man stared at us for a moment before stomping back toward his house. I shook my head. "Well, he was nice."

Clay laughed. "It's just a temporary metal stake. It's not like we're cutting down trees or even camping on his property."

"He asked a good question, though. How does it differentiate between fish and the bottom? Is it just because the fish move and the lake bottom doesn't?"

Clay nodded. "Pretty much. I'm sure it's a lot more complicated than that. One of the reasons we're doing multiple passes is to make sure it's the true bottom and not a fish."

"You really seem to know a lot about this stuff."

"Well, unlike someone I know, I was actually paying attention when Larkin described the project to me."

I stuck my tongue at Clay before facing forward. As he turned the boat, I pointed to the end of the cove. "You know, it's not that much further from the marker to the shore. Why don't we just map this whole area in one shot instead of moving the marker?"

"Works for me. The faster we get away from Mr. Grumpy, the better."

It took us less than an hour to map the cove and we moved the marker further downstream. The water was deeper than I expected and too dark to see anything beneath the surface. Some small boats sat near the center with their fishing lines dangling overboard. A fleeting thought crossed my mind: what type of bait would someone use to catch the water monster?

Mapping the lake itself took a lot longer than the river had. Because of its size, we swapped paddlers every five laps or so. It still took over three hours to map a single marker length. After moving the upstream stake downstream, we headed back to the campsite for an early lunch.

Since we weren't tracking, I set the transponder in the oar pocket and helped Clay paddle. Out of the corner of my eye, I could see his blade hitting the water at the same time as mine. We were a boat-length or two away from shore, where the water was definitely over our heads, when something struck the bottom of the boat.

We both stopped paddling instantly. I turned to Clay. "What was that?"

"I don't—"

Clay's eyes grew wide. I followed his gaze. Not far from us, in the deeper center of the lake, bubbles broke the surface as if the water was boiling. Beside it, a dark shape emerged. A rounded mound with sleek black skin. Before I could even register what was happening, the shape and bubbles came charging toward us.

Clay thrust his paddle in the water. "Let's get out of here!"

He didn't have to tell me twice. I dug into the water as quickly as I could. But, we weren't fast enough. The creature broadsided us so hard, the boat flipped over.

I instinctively held my breath and closed my eyes as I went under. Stilling my body, I could feel my life jacket bringing me back to the surface. I kicked in that direction, but something grabbed my leg. It started pulling me back down.

I opened my eyes, shutting them immediately when they started to burn. It was too blurry to see anything, although I thought I had seen a light. Perhaps it was the sun on the surface?

I tried to use my other senses. Something was wrapped around my ankle. The more I struggled, the tighter it seemed to grab.

My lungs were burning. I couldn't hold my breath much longer. Blackness seemed to envelope me. As I succumbed to it, I thought I could hear a faint whirring. Maybe a boat was coming to rescue me.

"Ellie! Talk to me! Come on!"

Clay's voice broke through my hazy brain. There was a weight on my sternum. I was laying on a flat surface. Something was in my throat. I felt like I was going to be sick.

I rolled to my side, letting the vomit come.

"*El Cafecito*! You're okay!"

I nodded, coughing out the remaining water. "What happened?"

I sat up slightly, looking around. Clay was kneeling beside me at the river's edge. He put an arm behind my back for support.

"Something hit the boat. We capsized. When I got to the surface, I couldn't find you. You were under for almost a minute. I was swimming toward your paddle when you finally came back up. I don't really know CPR, but I tried to do what they do on TV. Are you okay?"

I took a shaky breath. "I think so. Where are we?"

"I think it's the edge of the campground. I wasn't really paying attention."

I looked out at the lake. "What was that thing?"

"I have no idea. But, we're done for now. Let's get back to the campsite. Call Larkin. Then we'll go look for the boat."

Clay helped me to my feet. The world spun for a quick second, but I was okay. Using our paddles as walking sticks, we waded along the shore until we reached the first campsite. Since it was empty, we crossed through it to the path, quickly making our way to our own site. Clay pointed to the tent.

"Why don't you go rest?"

"I'm fine. Really. I can get lunch ready while you call Larkin."

Clay sighed. "I'm going to go get the boat first."

He gave me a quick kiss before walking to the water. I watched him wade in and swim away. I tried not to think about my near-drowning experience as I changed into dry clothes. After placing my wet ones on the picnic table, I searched the supply raft for today's cooler, grabbing the one from yesterday as well.

Because we had not used the stove, we were starting to accumulate extra food. I decided to cook the grilled cheese and soup for lunch. After being in the water, warm soup sounded perfect.

I angled myself on the picnic table in a way that enabled me to keep an eye on the lake. The kayak was not far from shore and Clay was able to swim to it easily. He left it upside down as he made his way back to our site. Since it seemed to follow him easily, I had a feeling he was holding it by the handle. That was how I would drag the boat if it were me.

Resting the pan of sandwiches on top of the pot of soup, I went to the water's edge to help Clay. Together, we pulled the boat ashore and examined the hull. There were no dents or dings. Not even a scuff mark. There was no evidence that anything had come in contact with the kayak.

We examined the tracking boat, but it had also remained unscathed. When we flipped the kayak right side up, I was relieved to see the transponder was still tucked safely in its pocket. Clay carried it to the picnic table.

"Maybe this thing caught something."

"Won't it think it's a fish? Because it was moving?"

"There is a fish-finder setting. I'll play with it over lunch."

"Maybe you can ask Larkin when we call him."

Clay frowned, disappearing into the tent while I filled our mugs with the soup. I couldn't blame him. I was not looking forward to contacting our boss either. After setting the transponder to upload its data, Clay placed the phone on the table between us. A moment later, Larkin answered.

"It's not raining. You better have a good reason for calling me while you're supposed to be on the water."

I saw the anger flash on Clay's face. "Something in the lake hit our boat and capsized us. Ellie nearly drowned."

Larkin swore. "Was the plotter damaged?"

I glared at the phone. "I'm fine, thanks."

Larkin scoffed. "Did you hit a rock?"

"No. Something rammed into us."

"Like a snapping turtle?"

I looked at Clay. "Snapping turtle?"

He shook his head. "This was much bigger and moved much faster."

Larkin didn't seem too concerned. "Is the boat damaged?"

"The boat's fine. Your tracker's fine. It wasn't even submerged. The data is uploading now."

I could hear Larkin let out a breath. "Okay. It's important to stick to our mission. If there's a creature under the water, we'll find it."

I narrowed my eyes. "Professor Larkin? I thought we were mapping the river, and the lake, to determine if it needed dredging."

"We are." I could hear the hesitation in Larkin's voice. "That's our primary goal. But, if the maps happen to show something else down there, well, that could be important, too. Now, it's almost noon. You have a quick lunch and get back out there."

Larkin ended the call without waiting for a response. Staring at the phone, I began to question whether my boss had been completely honest with me about this internship.

Chapter 8

I was very hesitant to return to the water after lunch. It was obvious *something* was in the lake. I still wasn't convinced it was a sea monster. But, I wasn't about to discredit the idea of a very fast snapping turtle. Or maybe a giant octopus.

Even though I insisted I was fine, Clay was adamant that he take the first paddling shift. As we headed toward the marker, I played with the settings on the transponder until it showed the fish beneath us. Thankfully, there were none.

As we moved into deeper water, the fish finder did show small creatures swimming beneath us. Though I was no expert, I was pretty sure none of them were larger than my hand. Maybe my forearm.

When I passed the tablet to Clay, he agreed with my assessment. As I scanned the shore to check for the markers, I would glance at the water in between. It remained undisturbed except for the ripples from our paddles.

We were still surveying the northern portion of the lake. Most of the activity seemed to be on the southern end. I watched people splashing around in the campground swimming area and fishermen casting lines on the opposite shore.

I didn't realize I had been staring until Clay's voice broke the silence.

"What does the fish finder say?"

I glanced at the display. I had forgotten to watch it. A large blob was swimming away from us.

I swore. "I see something!"

Clay stopped paddling, scooting forward to see for himself. "I don't see anything."

"It was there. I swear."

"I believe you." Clay placed a comforting hand on my shoulder. "But, it seems to have disappeared for now."

I took a deep breath, looking in the direction it had traveled. The water was still. Whatever I had seen was probably, hopefully, skimming the bottom.

We managed to complete two marker lengths by sunset, finishing just south of the campground swimming hole. After moving the marker, Clay insisted we map the swimming area. Since I hadn't forgotten the memory of something pulling me under, he volunteered.

We brought the kayak ashore just outside the swimming buoys, which were placed about six feet apart along a rope. Two children were splashing in the water while their parents sat on the sandy shore. They watched us with interest as Clay climbed out of the kayak and waded to the back. After he untethered the tracker boat, he dragged it to the buoys and pushed it over the rope.

The children sent Clay curious looks as he waded into the deeper water, pulling the boat behind him. The parents looked almost worried. When he could no longer touch the bottom, Clay swam to the end. Changing directions, he paddled two laps with the buoys beside him before moving to the next inland buoy. He repeated this until the water was shallow enough for him to walk. By the time he returned to the beach, the family had decided to go back to their site for dinner.

Clay dripped his way to me, clipping the tracker boat onto the kayak and sending me a mischievous smile.

"I'm going to walk back to the site so I don't get the kayak all wet. You think you can paddle back on your own?"

I nodded.

"Great. Last one there cooks. Ready? Go!"

He pushed the kayak into the water before turning and running toward the path. The swimming hole was on the opposite side of the campground and I knew Clay would have to weave along the roads to get there. My journey was much shorter. Yet somehow, he was waiting for me at the edge of the water, looking a little winded.

I narrowed my eyes at him. "How did you possibly beat me?"

"I . . . ran."

Since he was speaking between breaths, I wasn't surprised. After helping me pull the kayak ashore, he pranced to the tent.

"Since you're making supper, I'm going to take a shower. I

need to do laundry. Between falling in the lake earlier and taking a swim now, I have no more clean clothes."

Dinner didn't take too much time to prepare. The chicken was already cut into cubes. After cooking it in the pot, I added some vegetables, rice, and water. While it simmered, I built a fire and did my laundry at the river's edge.

I had just laid my clothes along the picnic table when Clay returned. I spooned the meal onto our plates as he dried his clothes, then we settled by the fire. He put his arm around me.

"This smells delicious. I'll make breakfast."

"No problem. How was your shower?"

"Very refreshing. So, did you upload the transponder data?"

I shook my head. "You need to do it on your phone."

Clay nodded, passing me his plate as he got to his feet. I balanced it in my lap, watching him grab the tablet and phone. After preparing the upload, he placed the plotter beside him, showing me his phone as he retrieved his plate.

"Look. The maps from this afternoon are up."

I raised my eyebrows. "Really? I thought they took like, a day or two."

Clay shrugged. "I guess not. Let's see if it can give us an idea of what attacked us."

I shuddered. I wasn't sure I *wanted* to know what had hit the boat. What had grabbed me. What had held me under, nearly drowning me.

I jumped to my feet. "I'm going to get changed."

Clay glanced at my plate. "You didn't finish eating."

"I'm not hungry."

"You have to eat. Replenish all the calories you lost today."

"I'll eat later. I'm not hungry."

I stormed into the tent a little angrier than I intended. Thankfully, Clay didn't try to follow me. I changed into my last clean shorts and shirt before curling into a ball on my bed, my back to the entrance. I wasn't tired. I just couldn't stop shaking.

"*El Cafecito*? You okay?"

Clay's voice was soft, but I was pretty sure he was standing by the tent flap. When I didn't answer, he crawled beside me, his arm around my waist.

"What's wrong?"

"Something pulled me under the water."

"Elver?"

The laughter in his voice made me angry. I rolled away,

glaring at him as I sat up.

"This isn't funny, Clay. Something grabbed me. Not some mythical sea creature. Something real."

"El, I wasn't trying to be funny. But think about this. We went back out *after* capsizing. Nothing attacked us then. The fish finder didn't see anything. Whatever it was, it's probably long gone."

I nodded, even though I wasn't convinced. There was something real in that water.

"Good. Now, can you come finish eating?"

I didn't respond. With a shrug, I crawled out of the tent. Clay spent the rest of the night telling me about his previous summer jobs while I picked at my food. When my plate was empty, I crawled into my sleeping bag, zipping it closed for the first time since we had arrived at the campsite.

Blackness surrounded me. I blinked, but that somehow made everything even darker. When I turned my body, I couldn't see a thing. But neither could I feel anything. My feet weren't on the ground. I wasn't lying on a surface. I was floating, drifting in the darkness.

In the distance, I heard a soft whirring. I reached in the direction I thought might be its source. I felt nothing.

Suddenly, something grabbed my waist. I tried to pull it away, but the more I struggled, the harder it held me. It tightened, squeezing until I couldn't breathe. I tried to scream, but no sound came. I kicked my legs and thrashed my body, hoping whatever was holding me would yield.

I sat up, gasping for air. My eyes shot open. I was in the tent. My sleeping bag was a twisted mess near my feet. Clay was sitting beside me, a look of panic on his face.

"El? Are you okay?"

My heart was racing and it took a minute for my breathing to return to normal. I nodded slowly.

"Yeah. It was just . . . a weird dream."

Clay ran his hand up and down my back. "Want to talk about it?"

I shook my head. "Not really."

"Okay. Why don't you come over here? Let me hold you."

I nodded, resting my head on his chest. He stroked my hair as

I closed my eyes. Focused on his heartbeat, I soon drifted back to sleep.

The sun was just beginning to rise when I woke in the morning. After a quick visit to the bathhouse, I decided I would make coffee before waking Clay. I set up the stove, filling the kettle with the melted ice in last night's cooler. While I waited for the water to boil, I scrambled some eggs in the pot.

The kettle whistled and I exchanged it for the pan on the burner. I threw in the ham and pre-cut vegetables, mixed them around a little, then poured in the eggs. I heard Clay stirring in the tent as I placed the food on our plates.

When I brought the pan to the water's edge for a quick wash, I happened to glance out at the lake. It was still as glass. Nothing was stirring. Except for a raft floating in its center. It looked a lot like our supply boat.

I surged to my feet. It *was* our supply boat.

"Clay! Get over here!"

"Hmm?" Clay emerged from the tent, rubbing sleep from his eyes. "What? Something wrong?"

I pointed out toward the lake. "The boat!"

Clay didn't bother covering his yawn. "Huh? Yeah. There's a boat out there. So?" Without waiting for a response, Clay started spooning coffee grounds into his mug.

I was losing my patience. Was he being this dense on purpose? I gestured to the trees where our raft had been. "Clay! It's *our* boat. The supply boat."

Clay stopped what he was doing. He looked between the trees and the lake a few times before swearing.

I shook my head. "Let's go get it before something happens to it."

Leaving the tracking boat on shore, we paddled the kayak toward the center of the lake. Clay spent the time trying to figure out what had happened.

"It's not like a wave came ashore and dragged it in the water."

"It was empty. Maybe a strong wind?"

Clay scoffed. "So, it survived the thunderstorm the other day, but a slight breeze blew it away? No. Someone had to have done this on purpose.”

“Why on earth would someone want to do that?”

“I have no idea. But, there’s no way this was an accident.”

Since I was facing forward, Clay couldn’t see me roll my eyes. “Maybe the lake monster came and grabbed it.”

“What’s with the sarcasm? I thought after yesterday, you of all people would believe there’s something in the lake.”

“But why steal the raft? Why not just attack us?”

Clay didn’t answer me as we pulled up along the raft. He grabbed the tether and clipped it onto the kayak. We were silent the entire way back to shore. As we approached our site, I realized the real reason someone would send our raft to the middle of the lake.

It gave that person a chance to trash our campsite. Food was thrown all over the area, the coolers having been tossed into the fire pit. Deep grooves gouged the bottom of the overturned picnic table. They matched the slash marks in the sides of the tent.

But, I hardly noticed the destruction. My eyes were glued to the splintered remains of the tracker boat.

“What exactly is going on here?”

I glanced toward the truck that had just parked along the road. Behind the police cruiser. Larkin looked ready to hurt someone.

The officer talking to Clay turned to him. “I’m sorry sir. This is a crime scene.”

Larkin pointed to the campsite. “That’s my property. I have a right to know what’s going on.”

Clay and I had already explained everything on the phone. It was Larkin’s idea to call the police. They were filing a report but weren’t sure what else we could do.

After receiving an update from the police, Larkin pointed to me and Clay. “I need to speak with you two.”

Clay ran a hand through his hair as we approached the truck. “Why would someone do this?”

“I might have an idea.” Larkin opened the passenger door and retrieved a laptop, which he placed on the hood. As soon as it booted to life, I recognized the mapping software we were using with the chartplotter.

“This is the data from yesterday. As you can see, this area

near the mouth has a lot of sediment. It's much shallower than the rest of the lake."

Clay scoffed. "So, it needs dredging. That doesn't explain why someone would trash our site."

"Can you think of a reason why someone wouldn't want us to dredge?"

As Clay shook his head, I looked past our campsite to the lake. A number of boaters were out today. Many were looking at our site. More were rowing back and forth along the center of the lake.

I turned back to Larkin. "There's a lot of people out today. Are they all looking for Elver?"

He nodded. "I think so. There's been a lot of stories about the man who drowned last weekend. There have been more stories."

Clay sent Larkin an incredulous look. "So, you think the lake monster tore apart our campsite?"

Larkin responded so quietly, Clay and I had to lean in to better hear him. "I think someone wants you to *think* the lake monster did it."

Chapter 9

"Why does this feel like a punishment?"

I smiled at Clay sitting at the computer beside me. "We're lucky we still have jobs. Besides, look at the bright side. No more roughing it."

He sighed, clicking his mouse before turning back to me. "I know. But, making a spreadsheet of historic water depths? My eyes are bleeding."

"It's better than searching online archives for references to the river. Do you know how many people have reported sightings of Elver?"

"How many?"

I shrugged. "I stopped counting. But, I mean, these go back to colonial days. I found one from 1652."

Clay leaned over to look at my screen. "Really? They called it Elver?"

"Nah. It just described the strange serpent a bunch of sailors saw in the lake while they were traveling up the river."

"What lake? Where we were?"

I nodded. "Early colonists used to use the river to trade fur with the natives and other colonists from the Sound up through to Canada."

Clay typed something on his computer. A moment later, a satellite image of the river appeared on his screen. He zoomed in until it showed the portion from the lake to ocean, then pointed to the middle of the display.

"How did they get past Rattlesnake falls?"

"Wait a sec. I read something about that."

I dug through the piles of books beside me. Over the past

three days, I had searched many titles. But, the name Rattlesnake Falls had stuck in my head.

It took a few minutes, but I found the book containing the newspaper article dated April 1908. I showed it to Clay.

Rattlesnake Falls Dam
Finishes Construction

He read the article silently before turning to me. "So, boats used to just pass right through the area?"

I nodded. "Yeah. Until the Revolutionary War, at least. The main trading company lost a bunch of ships and went out of business."

"Lost ships?"

"Yeah. During the war, the colonists sank a lot of the ships. There's one they never found. The *Otter*. It was making its way up north with a ton of gold and treasures for trading. Reports show it entered the lake but never left."

I turned back to the report I had been typing for Larkin. "The last reference I found to the boat was in 1805. A fisherman found a crate of glass beads, stamped with the name of the trading company that owned the *Otter*."

The slamming of the fire door in the hallway had Clay jumping back to his computer. A moment later, Larkin stepped into the room, rubbing his hands together in excitement as he sat on the desk behind us.

"Okay, kids. I just heard from my boat guy. He fixed up the tracking boat enough that we can use it."

I raised my eyebrows. "Really? Doesn't that take, like, months to build?"

"Well, it's not really a boat anymore. More like a raft. You'll see it tomorrow when you go back to the lake."

Clay pointed to his computer. "What about these reports?"

Larkin waved a dismissive hand. "Oh, they'll be waiting for you when you're done with the maps. You can work on them during the fall semester if you have to."

I sat a little straighter in my chair. "Really? We're working for you in the fall?"

"Sure. I could use a couple lab assistants. My budget for next year was cleared. But, back to the issue at hand. You guys are going back to the lake."

He called up an image of the map on his phone, turning the

display for me and Clay to see. He pointed to the campground. "Your map data goes to about here. I need you to finish the lake with your north-south measurements. Then, I want you to start at the southern end and work your way back north. Going east-west." He made a horizontal zigzag from the bottom of his screen to the top. "But, I want you to work in nice, tight lines so we get a lot of overlap. I want that map to be as precise as possible."

Clay sent Larkin a confused look. "Do we have to do that for the entire river? Because there were some spots so narrow, I don't think we *could* turn the kayak sideways."

Larkin shook his head. "No. Right now, we're going to focus on the lake. Ellie, tell me what you learned about it."

I gave him a brief summary of my report, ending with the sunken trading boat. Larkin's eyes grew wide with excitement. "And *that's* why we're going to go into so much detail. We're going to see if we can figure out where this boat is. So it's not damaged when we dredge."

Clay sent me a sideways glance. I knew he was thinking the same as me. I doubted Larkin's interest in the boat was related to the dredging.

The following morning, Larkin helped Clay secure the kayak to the roof of his car. Since we were planning on staying much longer than a day, Larkin insisted we get our own provisions instead of him bringing us coolers every few days. I didn't mind. I wouldn't be stuck in the hump seat for nearly two hours.

Larkin had reserved the same site we had used previously. Since it was unoccupied, he had even gotten us permission to set up in the morning, instead of waiting until the afternoon check-in time. I was glad to see that all evidence of our attack had been removed. Sure, there were probably still gouges underneath the table, but as long as I didn't see them, I could pretend they weren't there. After carrying the kayak to the shore, Clay turned to me.

"Why don't you unload the car while I set up the tent. Just put everything on the table and we can sort through it later."

I shrugged, passing him the tent bundle. Since we weren't breaking it down every night, Larkin had supplied us with a more permanent structure. Clay got to work as I pulled everything out of the trunk. He was still fighting with the poles when the car was empty. I set up our camp chairs and a drying rack by the fire, as well as the pop-up tent over the picnic table, before going to his side.

"Would you like a hand?"

Clay swore. "I think there's a piece missing."

I kissed his cheek. "Why don't you go make lunch while I do this."

"Good luck."

I didn't need luck. I had been camping more times than I could count. I had the tent ready before Clay could find the subs we had picked up on our way to the campground. While we ate, we tossed our belongings into the tent and set up the double air mattress he had brought. Clay huffed out a breath as he stowed the trash in the car.

"We have just enough time, I think, to do two lengths of the lake. Ready?"

I picked up my life jacket. "Let's get to it."

The tracker was no longer in a boat. Larkin's guy had cut out a section a little larger than a kickboard, rounded the edges, and attached a pool noodle around the perimeter. It resembled a strange doughnut with an even stranger center.

While Clay paddled to the edge of the campground's swimming area, I carried the orange markers through the camp. I was surprised to see so many sites occupied. When I reached the beach, I expected to see a lot of people in the water. There were, but most of them were in boats out in the middle of the lake. I placed the first stake just south of the swimming area and waded along the shore until I ran out of chain.

As I secured the second stake, Clay pulled up alongside me. "Climb aboard. Just like in the pool."

I glared at his smirk. Thankfully, the shore was higher than it had been on the ramp. Steadying the boat with my hand, I was able to reach my foot over the side and onto the seat. Pressing all my weight on that leg, I stood. My intention was to turn around and sit gracefully.

Unfortunately, that was not what happened. I stood too quickly, losing my balance. My arms flailed in the air as I went over the opposite side of the boat.

The water was about knee-deep. I had no problem getting to

my feet. Which was a good thing, since Clay was laughing too hysterically to be of any assistance. I glared at him while I marched angrily around the boat back to the shore.

"This is your fault. You jinxed me."

"Has it occurred to you, maybe it's you?"

I pulled the boat toward me until it was nearly touching the bottom. This time, I was able to climb in with ease. Grabbing the transponder from its pocket, I turned to Clay.

"I'm still blaming you. Ready?"

Still laughing, Clay pushed us away from shore while I set up the tablet to collect our afternoon data.

As Clay paddled, I watched the tourists in the water. Some were in kayaks while others were in small boats. Nearly everyone was fishing, though a few looked to be using large nets instead of poles. Most of them were near the center of the lake.

Right where Clay and I needed to paddle. We did our best to go around them, but our map was full of jagged lines in both directions. I was pretty sure there would be some serious holes when we uploaded the data that night.

I wasn't sure about Clay, but whenever I was holding the transponder, I was actively scanning for anything under the water. Some of the fish were larger than my foot, but the display showed nothing that could be mistaken for a sea monster. Despite the abundant submarine life, however, I rarely saw any of the fishermen catching anything. Of course, they blamed their poor luck on us.

An elderly man in a canoe yelled at Clay as we passed. "You're scaring away all the fish!"

"Yeah!" The man in the next kayak nodded eagerly. "How we supposed to catch Elver?"

The first man shook his head. "There's no lake monster. Just a bunch of trout. Which you lot are scaring away."

I wanted to explain how we were doing important government research and that dredging the lake could result in greater numbers of fish surviving the winter. However, Clay had already glided us out of earshot, so I had to keep my comments to myself.

By the time we finished the second section of the lake, even more boaters had taken to the water. We had to navigate around them just to get back to our campsite. I groaned I started the campfire.

"Larkin's going to make us redo the data, isn't he?"

Clay frowned. "I hope not. I'll upload it, but I'm going to wait for him to mention it. Maybe, once we add in the data from the other direction, there will be enough information to satisfy him."

"Think we're going to find the missing boat? The *Otter*?"

Clay laughed. "I think we have a better chance of catching Elver."

That night, we grilled burgers and fresh corn over the fire while enjoying our cold beers. As the fire dimmed, we watched the stars appear over the lake. The people in the neighboring site were still partying with their loud music when Clay and I turned in for the night.

I was at the bottom of the lake, digging with a shovel while trout circled around me, when I realized I had to pee. As I swam to the underwater portable restroom, I blinked a few times.

It took me a moment to focus. I wasn't underwater. I was in my tent, snuggled under a blanket with Clay. And I really did have to pee. With a resigned sigh, I crawled out of the tent. The bathhouse was too far away to walk in the middle of the night. I went to the spot where we used to keep the supply boat, a little wooded area not far from the water's edge.

When I was done, I happened to glance at the lake before returning to the tent. There was a strange glow near the center, not far from where the old man had accosted us that afternoon. I moved closer to the edge to get a better look.

The light was emanating from the lake itself. Something *under the water* was producing it. Professor Larkin had taught us about some sea creatures that created their own light to attract prey. But, they lived at depths far deeper than this lake. Surely, I wasn't seeing one of those.

Something moved near the light. I couldn't make out the shape, but it was definitely a dark shadow. And it was a lot bigger than a trout. I ran back to the tent. Clay's warmth helped me forget about my mysterious sea creature.

Chapter 10

The next morning morning, I noticed a large clump of boats while I was paddling. They were not far from where I had seen the mysterious light. I pointed it out to Clay.

"See where all those people are gathered?"

I glanced behind me in time to see him look up from the transponder and squint toward the mass of people.

"Yeah. What about it?"

"Last night, I got up in the middle of the night to pee."

Clay chuckled. "You're going to tell me that's where you went?"

"No, but I was dreaming that there was a bathroom underwater. When I got up, it was like two or three in the morning. Everything was dead quiet. But, there was this light in the lake. Underwater. And I could see something swimming near it. Something big. And that light? It was right around where all those boats are now."

"You think it was Elver?"

I could hear the humor and skepticism in Clay's voice and I caught a glimpse of him as I turned the boat. He clearly didn't believe me.

I was annoyed that he was being so flippant about what I had seen. I was frustrated that he wasn't taking my concerns so seriously. Had he already forgotten that something had rammed into us less than a week ago?

I frowned. "There's no sea monster. But, there is *something* under the lake. A big something."

"With a light. You think it's an angler fish? At this depth?"

I rolled my eyes, even though Clay couldn't see me. "Obviously not. I have no idea what it is."

Clay didn't respond and I paddled in silence for a while. I still didn't believe that a sea creature lived in the lake. But, I was starting to think that maybe something was there. An idea began to form in my mind. I waited until I turned the boat again before voicing my theory aloud.

"Hey, Clay?"

"Mmm?"

"Last week, there was only like, a handful of people here, right?"

"Yeah, I guess."

"If someone wanted to look underwater for a sunken boat, they could do it during the day, right?"

"Maybe. I mean, you can't really see much in this lake. It's so murky."

"What if they found a way around it. Then, they can spend their day combing the lake, a lot like we're doing with the tracker. But then, all these people started showing up, and now they can't look during the day."

I glanced at Clay to see if he was following my train of thought. He nodded. "Yeah. They'd probably swim into all the boats."

"Or get caught in a fishing line. So then, if they wanted to search, they'd have to wait until nighttime."

"So, you think you saw someone swimming with a flashlight searching for treasure?"

"Pretty much. Yeah."

Clay shook his head with a smile. "I still like the idea of a glowing sea monster, but your theory sounds a little more reasonable."

We worked until the sun went down, taking only a few small breaks. By the time we pulled the boat out of the water for the evening, we had mapped most of the lake. There was only a little more than one section left.

Before going to bed, I set an alarm to wake me around two in the morning. I wanted to see if the mysterious light returned. I almost didn't hear it, however. It's sound was drowned out by a passing thunderstorm.

With a sigh, I rolled over and went back to sleep.

Saturday morning, when Clay and I finished mapping the lake, we rowed to its southernmost part. After aligning the boat, Clay worked the transponder while I rowed to the east shore. Turning around for the next lap, I tried to align the boat with our own wake. The last thing I wanted was for Larkin to make us do this all over again because our lines weren't tight enough.

After about ten laps, Clay switched jobs with me. While I had the transponder, I would occasionally look toward the fishermen. There were fewer people out today. Even though it was well past breakfast, the sun had decided to stay behind the clouds. By the time Clay was ready for a rest, it was actually getting too dark to see. Glancing at the sky, I turned around to hand him the tablet.

"Hey, Clay? Do you think maybe we should head back to the campsite?"

"Why? You see something in the water?"

In answer to my question, thunder rumbled in the distance. I pointed upwards. "That's why."

Clay waved a dismissive hand. "Ah, the storm's still far away. I didn't even see the lightning."

I was halfway to the east shore when lightning brightened the sky. Two strokes later, thunder followed. I didn't even bother turning around.

"Now can we go back?"

I heard Clay sigh. "Fine. But, row to shore first. I want to put the markers where we stopped."

He placed both stakes in the ground—one in front of the other—and hopped back into the boat. Together, we rowed toward the campsite. We had just removed the boat from the water when the skies opened.

We ran under the dining tent, although it didn't provide us with much protection against the weather. Together, we lowered it until it was just higher than the picnic table. Sitting shoulder to shoulder on the bench, we were able to stay somewhat dry while we made some peanut butter sandwiches.

I smirked as I bit into mine. "So, I guess we're done for the day?"

Clay shrugged. "You know Larkin wants us out there in the rain. But, yeah. We're done at least til the storm passes."

"Good. I want to get out of these wet clothes."

He ran his hand along my arm. "Well, since you suggested it, would you like some help?"

The storm lasted into the evening. I wasn't sure what Clay was doing on his phone, but I spent a lot of my afternoon searching for news reports about Elver Lake. I wanted to know why so many people were suddenly interested in fishing. I thought maybe there was a derby or that the lake had been stocked. But, the only reports I could find suggested the increase in traffic was due to people wanting to capture the monster.

After supper, I decided to take Clay up on his offer to help me out of my clothes. We were up late, but I had no trouble falling asleep naked in his arms. I was rudely awakened a couple of hours later when my alarm sounded.

"What's that?" Clay sat up, rubbing the sleep from his eyes.

I quickly silenced the alarm. "I'm sorry. Go back to sleep. I didn't realize that was still on."

Clay lay back down, twirling a lock of my hair. "But, why did you set it in the first place?"

I was glad it was dark. I could feel the heat rising to my cheeks. "I wanted to see if that weird light was under the lake again. I set it yesterday, but it was raining. I must have forgotten to disable it."

Clay kissed me. "Well, now that I'm awake, I'm going to the men's room." He started to crawl toward the door.

I slapped his rear end lightly. "You may want to cover that up before you go out there."

We quickly threw on clothes and walked together to the bathhouse. The campground was silent. I could hear water dripping from the trees and a few people snoring, but no other noise.

Clay was waiting for me when I exited the bathroom. Hand in hand, we meandered back to the campsite. As we circled the tent to the flap, I glanced at the lake.

"Look!" My whisper sounded loud in the stillness of the evening. Clay glanced where I was pointing and swore under his breath.

"What is that?"

"No clue."

We moved to the water's edge to get a better look. As we stared, the light swam closer to shore faster than humanly possible. A trail of air bubbles followed in its wake. Clay kicked off his flip-flops and waded into the water. I called out to him in a whisper.

"Can you see where it's going?"

"It's headed toward the mou—no. It turned. It's going toward the east bank. Ugh."

Clay shook his head as he returned to land. "Lost it at the last second. I can show you in the morning. I think I know where I last saw it."

I pointed in the opposite direction. "We're supposed to work."

"If you're okay with oatmeal for breakfast, we can set out early, look at where I saw the creature."

I frowned. "You don't seriously believe it's Elver."

"No. I just don't know what else to call it."

"Fair." I looked around. "So, now what? It's too early to be awake, but I am too awake to go back to bed."

Clay grabbed my hand, pulling me toward the tent with a smile. "Oh, I have a few ideas that might work."

We woke at dawn, boiling water as we gathered our things for the day. After a very quick breakfast of oatmeal and coffee, we put the kayak into the water and headed upstream.

Although the sky was pink, the sun had not risen enough to illuminate the lake. Paddling in the darkness felt strange, like I was dreaming.

Clay navigated, leading us toward a familiar house. It was difficult to see with the sun almost directly behind it, but I was pretty sure I knew where we were. I turned to Clay.

"Isn't this where that guy yelled at us?"

Clay turned the boat as if we were going to climb out. "Maybe? Yeah, I think you're right."

Thankfully, the man was not there to yell at us again. I glanced in the water on my other side. "Why do you think the light creature came here?"

"Maybe so Mr. Curmudgeon could yell at him?"

Clay laughed at his own joke, but I didn't. I was too busy staring at the bottom of the lake. It was shallower here, about chest deep. And the dawn was just bright enough to reflect on something bright blue shining on the bottom.

"Hang on a sec. I want to try something." I kicked off my shoes and climbed onto the shore.

Clay raised his eyebrows. "What are you doing?"

"I saw something. I want to grab it."

Sitting on the ground, I put my feet in the water. It was colder than I expected, but not too unpleasant. I slid all the way in, trying not to think about the fact that my feet were sinking into the squishy bottom. I took large steps, hoping to displace as little silt as possible.

I tried to capture the blue object between my toes, failing miserably and nearly burying it in the sand. I quickly withdrew my foot, squatting as I waited for the sand to settle. I lined up my hand, took a deep breath and closed my eyes.

It took a little groping, but my hand wrapped around something smooth. Grasping it tightly, I returned to the surface.

"Got it!"

"WHAT ARE YOU DOING?"

Wiping the water from my eyes, I turned to see the grouchy man racing down the bank toward us. Thinking quickly, I shoved my treasure into my pocket and pulled off my sunglasses as I walked back to the shore.

The irate man reached the boat as I was climbing back in.

"This is private property! What do you think you're doing?"

I held up my sunglasses, sending him the most apologetic smile I could muster. "I'm so sorry. I was so upset last night, I couldn't sleep. I lost my favorite sunglasses. The ones that used to belong to my grandmother. They fell off when I was looking for fish yesterday, but I couldn't see them. It was so dark, you know? So this morning, since it was so much clearer, we decided to try looking for them. And look. I found them."

"Well, then what are you still doing here?"

Clay pushed us away from the shore. "Sorry, sir. Why don't we go check out the other part of the lake this morning?"

The man glared at us. "I think that's an excellent idea."

Chapter 11

Clay and I stopped at the campsite long enough for me to change into dry clothes. I took an extra minute to examine my treasure.

The royal blue sphere was about the size of a blueberry, almost glowing as light shone through it. A hole in the center suggested it might belong to a necklace. Instinct told me it was made of glass, like the beads the colonists used to trade with the natives.

I quickly shoved the ball into the side pocket of my pack and returned to the kayak. By the time we reached our starting point for the day, I had forgotten about it.

We paddled along the lake continuously until well past noon. Eventually, we ran out of snacks, and energy, and decided to take a lunch break. We had just reached our dining tent when dark clouds filled the sky and a light rain began to fall. It was enough to have most of the boaters leave the lake. I groaned.

"If it keeps raining, we're never going to finish this project. Larkin will have us out here every weekend all semester."

Clay smiled. "I bet the river could freeze and he would still want us chartplotting."

"And probably not pay us until it's done."

"Then I say we go earn our paycheck."

"What? Go out in the rain?"

Clay shrugged. "Why not? There's no thunder and it's not raining all that much. Plus, everyone else left. We'd have the place to ourselves."

I frowned, glancing at the sky. "Fine. But, first sign of thunder, we stop."

"Deal."

Clay and I took full advantage of not having to maneuver around other boaters. Pushing ourselves to our limits, we were able to row faster, nearly reaching the middle of the lake by suppertime.

Although the rain had lessened, it was still soaking my clothes. When my teeth started to chatter, I decided we had better stop for the night.

"Cl-Clay? C-Can w-we g-g-g-go b-b-back?"

Clay swore. "El! Why didn't you say something sooner?"

I was too cold to paddle, so Clay did all the work. I just thought about getting into my bed.

The strange light in the water appeared under us out of nowhere. One moment everything was dark and the next, our boat was sitting on a glowing oasis. Instinctively, I looked over the edge. Maybe I could finally see something in the darkness.

A shadow. A shadow was definitely coming toward us. It had a bulbous head with lots of bubbles emanating from its mouth. I sat up quickly.

"Clay! Something's coming at us!"

I grabbed my paddle, but it was too late. The creature rammed against us.

My scream echoed across the lake as I fell out of the boat. The water was warmer than the air and for a moment, I stopped shivering. Then, something grabbed my leg.

My first thought, before I even had a chance to freak out, was "Oh man! Not again." It was almost immediately replaced with fear.

I tried to kick free, but I couldn't escape the creature's grip. The light was gone, but it felt almost like a human hand was grabbing me around the ankle. I guessed where a face might be and kicked.

The hand didn't free me. It gripped tighter as it dragged me across the lake at lightning speed. My head dipped underwater. I strained to break the surface long enough to gasp for air before being pulled under again.

The creature slowed and I dared to open my eyes. Something was crawling onto the shore ahead of me. It had long, webbed feet and a sleek black body. When it turned back to the shore, I could see a single eye reflected in the limited light.

It reached into the water, dragging Clay ashore by his life jacket. He wasn't moving and I feared he might have drowned. As the horrible creature rose up on two legs, I worried for Clay. When it turned toward me, it did the scariest thing imaginable.

It spoke.

Its voice was gruff and gravelly, but there was something familiar about it. I knew for certain I had heard it before, but I wasn't sure where. Despite the familiarity, I had trouble understanding its words.

"Whash wok?"

I didn't get a chance to ask it to repeat itself. The second creature, the one holding me, passed me to the first one. It climbed out as the first one dragged me beside Clay. I tried to keep my head up so I wouldn't hit any rocks.

The second creature crawled ashore, crouching low for a moment before standing on his back legs. Although I was watching upside down, it looked like it was walking toward me on human feet. Before I could confirm my suspicions, everything went dark.

I awoke in a dark room. A tiny amount of light fought its way through a tattered curtain dressing a window far above me. My head hurt. I tried to press it, but my hands were tied behind my back.

A chill went through me and I started shivering, unable to stop. My clothes, while not soaked, were still damp. The floor I was lying on was cold and hard, like concrete.

I tried to stand, but my legs were also tied. I settled for rolling in all directions until I found Clay.

He was nearby, his hands and legs bound as mine were. I rolled until I was beside him, his body warm enough to quell my shivering while I nudged him with my head.

"Clay! Wake up!" I kept my voice low. I had no idea where our captors might be.

He moaned as he rolled to face me. "What happened?"

"I don't know. Something hit the boat. Dragged us ashore."

"Elver?"

"Can Elver stand on two legs and talk? Can Elver tie us up and throw us in what I assume is a basement?"

Clay sent me a confused look. "Huh?"

I shook my head. "Never mind. My point was, I think people

tied us up. We have to get out of here."

A loud noise overhead had me rolling away from Clay. A moment later, a bright light shone as someone hustled down the stairs.

"Oh, good. You're awake."

I recognized the gruff voice. And the man attached to it. It was the old fisherman who had yelled at us the other day.

I glared at him. "What do you want?"

"Well, I'm not going to kill you, if that's what you're worried about. I just want information."

"What kind of information?" Clay's voice sounded weak. I spared him a glance. He had rolled to face our captors, but his lips were nearly blue.

The old man must have seen it, too. He picked up a thick blue blanket, the kind found in a moving truck, and tossed it at Clay. "Here. Get yourself warm. Tell us what we want to know, and you can go back to taking pictures of the fish."

"We weren't—"

The man put up a hand. "I don't care what you were doing. I just want to see the pictures. Where is the *Otter*?"

I didn't know how to answer. Clay beat me to it. "The otters? I'm not sure I saw any. The chartplotter just kind of shows us blobs when there's a fish. It doesn't identify them. But, I don't know much about otters. Don't they prefer shallower water? Like upriver?"

The man kicked Clay in the ribs so hard, I could almost feel the sting myself. Clay doubled over with pain as the man crouched down to look him in the eye.

"Think you're being funny? I don't do funny. Tell me what you know."

Clay didn't respond right away. When he did, his voice was strained. "Nothing."

This seemed to be the wrong answer. The man stepped to me, grabbing my arm and yanking me to my feet. "I said I wasn't going to kill you. But, if you don't cooperate, I might have to hurt this pretty girlfriend of yours." He removed a knife from his back pocket, flicking the blade open with a practiced ease. He ran the tip along my arm. "How about I carve your name in her flesh? Would that help you remember?"

I tried to pull free, but the man strengthened his grip. I looked at him, hoping he would see the honesty in my words.

"Please! I'm the one that knows about the *Otter*. I researched it. Clay was responsible for looking at historic depth charts."

The man jerked me around to face him. "Where is it?"

I shook my head. "I-I don't know. I swear. All I know is that it was lost in the lake."

"And that contraption of yours?"

"What contraption?"

"That computer you two have been playing around with in the water. The one you told my brother takes pictures of the lake. Did you see any pictures of the treasure while you were rowing back and forth?"

"It doesn't really take pictures. It's sonar."

"Dennis! Get up here!" I recognized the voice at the top of the stairs as belonging to the grumpy man who didn't want us on his property.

Dennis threw me back onto the floor with a grunt. "Idiot."

Clay tried to sit up. "Hey!"

"Relax. I was talking about my brother. He's the idiot. This whole mess is his fault."

As soon as Dennis disappeared, I crawled over to Clay. "Are you okay?"

He groaned. "No. But, I'm going to pretend I am."

I did my best to cover him with the blanket, although I couldn't see my hands. "We're going to get out of here."

"Turn around. Let me try to untie your hands."

Clay didn't get a chance as footfalls again sounded on the stairs. I did my best to sit up against a wall. I had absolutely no experience being a hostage, but according to every television show and movie I had ever watched, the more I could get the guy to talk, the better chance I had of being rescued. And if I wanted to stall, I needed to be sitting. Especially when I saw that Mr. Curmudgeon was the one who had come to join us.

"Start talking."

"Um, okay. I don't think we've been introduced. My name is Ellie—"

"Shut up! I want to know what you know about the treasure."

"Nothing."

"Why were you in front of my property yesterday? And don't give me some stupid story about your sunglasses."

"We thought, we thought we saw something during the night. It was coming here. We went exploring."

"What did you find? You were in the water. What did you find?"

"A-a bead. A glass bead."

"The two of you seem to be spending a lot of time combing through the lake. What other treasures have you seen?"

"Nothing. I swear. We're just mapping the floor. Can we go now?"

The man sent me a smile so evil, chills went down my spine. "Go? And where would you go?"

"Well, for starters, I would probably bring Clay to the emergency room. He's not looking so good."

The man nodded slowly. "Yes. He probably could use a doctor. Let's make a deal. Why don't you tell me what you know, and you can bring your boyfriend to the hospital."

"What do you want to know?"

"Everything you know about the *Otter*."

I bit my lower lip. "Well, the *Otter* was one of the biggest boats owned by the *Elver River Trading Company*. In seventeen—"

The man kicked Clay in nearly the exact spot Dennis had. I screamed. Clay grunted and again doubled over.

The man sneered in my direction. "Let's not be cute."

"I don't know what you mean. You asked about the *Otter*. I was telling you what I know."

"I didn't ask for a history lesson. I want to know what you know about its location."

"It's here. In the lake. But, I swear, I don't know where. I already told—"

"Well, you better figure out where it is. Or your boyfriend here may not live long enough to get to that doctor."

He kicked Clay one more time before going up the stairs. I heard the door slam and the lights went out. As my eyes adjusted to the dimness, I checked on Clay.

"Are you okay?"

He couldn't respond with anything more than a groan. I looked all around. In the opposite corner of the room was a pile of white shavings under a wooden workbench.

Although I knew nothing on television was real, I tried to wriggle my hands around my legs like I had seen in some movie or other. I nearly pulled my arm out of my socket, but I managed to get my hands in front of me. Quickly, I tried to untie my ankles, but I couldn't loosen the rope.

I walked across the floor on my knees, as quickly as I dared without damaging my kneecap. As I approached, I saw a small hand saw. I grabbed it, pulling my feet in front of me. After propping the saw—blade up—between my knees, I pulled my hands as far apart as I could and ran the rope between them across the blade.

It felt like forever, but I managed to free my hands. After liberating my feet, I ran to Clay and removed his ties as well. I had just finished when the basement light flicked on.

Chapter 12

I quickly sat against the wall, my feet in front of me, and threw the blanket over us, making sure the saw was hidden between me and Clay. As someone descended the staircase, I remembered to place my hands behind me for good measure.

A man I didn't recognize stood before us. He looked pained to even be there. He glanced up the stairs before whispering to us.

"Are you two okay?"

"Not really. We're being held hostage. My boyfriend keeps getting beat up because we don't know anything about some missing treasure."

The man ran his hands through his hair. "Oh, this is all my fault. I was fishing. Nearly a year ago. Snagged my line. When I finally reeled it in, it was caught in a wooden plank. On the side it said *Elver River Trading Company*. I showed it to my brother. He looked it up on his computer. Found out about the missing ship."

I sent him a curious look. "If you know where the boat is, why are you keeping us?"

The man started pacing. "That's just it. We *don't* know where it is. I thought I knew where I found the crate, but we can't find it anymore. Then, my brother got Mike involved. Said he would fund the project if we shared the treasure with him."

"What went wrong?"

The man shook his head. "Everything. We spent six months designing the light blocking shell so we could search underwater without being seen. But someone did see us and resurrected that stupid lake monster story. Now the lake is too full of tourists for us to get anything done. We have to wait until nighttime. Then, my idiot brother rams into some random night fisherman."

"The guy who drowned last week?"

The man nodded. "I swear, it was an accident. My brother rammed into the boat and knocked the guy out. Dennis panicked and tried to get back to shore, but he didn't realize the guy's foot was stuck in the shell. Ended up dragging him underwater for the length of the lake. By the time my brother surfaced, the guy was unconscious."

"So, you called 9-1-1?"

The man shook his head. "No. Dennis brought the man to the opposite shore, down where the lake exits back into the river. Left him in the reeds. Didn't even report it. Let someone else find the body in the morning."

"You could have called the authorities." I glared at the man. I felt absolutely no sympathy for him.

"I would have, but my brother didn't tell me what had happened until after the body had been discovered."

"You still could have told someone what had happened."

The man sent me a pained look. "I wanted to. I really did. But, Mike wouldn't let us. He said we were making too many mistakes and he was taking charge. He insisted we use the shell and search during the day again. Then, you kids showed up with your fancy tracker. Mike thought you were trying to find the treasure for yourself."

"We want to dredge the lake."

The man held up his hands in defense. "I know. But, Mike thinks you're lying. That's why he rammed into you last week. Held you under for a minute to make you think you were being attacked by a sea monster. It's why he trashed your campsite. Broke your little boat. He was trying to get you guys to leave."

I shrugged. "Well, it worked."

The man sent me a humorless smile. "Yeah, but you came back. When Mike saw you yesterday, he almost grabbed you then. Dennis convinced him to wait and see what you were up to. Went fishing to see if he could get any information. Your story hadn't changed, so I told everyone I didn't think you two knew about the treasure. But, Mike wasn't convinced."

"How'd he know we'd be on the water during the storm?"

"That was luck. We were planning how to kidnap you and Dennis saw you out on the lake in the rain. Mike figured using the shell would be perfect. It hid the light until they were under you. Then, they were able to knock you out of the boat and bring you here."

"What happens now? We really don't know anything."

The man sighed. "I know. That's why they sent me down here. To kill you."

He said it so emotionlessly, I thought he was kidding. I didn't react as he came beside us. Crouching low, he grabbed my chin, forcing me to look at him.

I found the saw, but by the time I gripped it, the man had already turned to Clay with an evil smile.

"I think I'll kill him first. Let you watch."

I threw the blanket away and whacked the man with the saw. I was hoping to cut him, but I ended up hitting him with the handle. It bounced off him.

However, the action gave me the opportunity to scurry away. I ran across the room to the workbench. A white plastic pipe was laying on the floor. Wielding it like a baseball bat, I swung at the man's face as he charged at me.

The man spun in a nearly complete circle before landing on the floor. I didn't realize I had such a powerful swing. It must have been from all the paddling I had been doing.

I rushed back to Clay. He was still unconscious. As painful as it was to leave him behind, I knew there was no way I could escape with him. I gave him a quick kiss.

"I'll be back. I promise."

Standing on the workbench, I could just barely reach the window with the tattered curtain. I yanked it aside and pushed out the screen. With a deep breath, I jumped up, reaching out the window and grabbing the sill. I scaled the wall as I pushed my head, then torso through the tiny window.

I could hear moaning from inside the basement. I wasn't sure who it was, but telling myself it was the guy who wanted to kill me provided me with the burst of energy I needed to push my hips through the window.

I crawled on my belly until I could scramble to my feet, then ran straight across the yard into the trees.

I didn't stop running until I reached the neighboring house. Panting, I frantically knocked on the door. There was no answer. I ran around the back, but there was no other entry. There was, however, a large window just beside the front door.

I grabbed the biggest rock I could find and smashed the window, trying to break away the jagged pieces and make a hole large enough to climb through. Inside, I found a phone immediately. I grabbed the handset and ran further into the house as I called the police.

"9-1-1. What's your emergency?"

"Someone is trying to kill me."

"What's your address, miss?"

I ran into a bedroom, straight to a closet. Closing the door, I huddled in a corner, I tried to answer the dispatcher as I fought to catch my breath.

"I-I don't know. I ran away. Broke into the neighbor's house. No one's home."

I heard a noise in the hallway. I lowered my voice to a whisper. "He followed me. You have to hurry!"

I hung up before the dispatcher could respond. My roommate had a cell phone that accidentally dialed 9-1-1 in her purse. More than once. Each time, police tracked her down to make sure she was not in trouble. I hoped that worked with landlines as well.

I strained my ears, listening for the slightest noise. All I could hear was the blood rushing in my ears as my heart pumped in overdrive. When I heard sirens in the distance, I let out a breath I hadn't realized I was holding. But, I still didn't move.

"Ellie? Can you hear me? It's the police. I know you called us. You can come out now."

Relieved, I got to my feet. My hand was on the door when I realized I had never told the police my name.

I searched the closet for something—anything—I could use to defend myself. I found an umbrella, but there was no way I would be able to swing it in such a small space. I could jab it, but that wouldn't be very effective.

Unless it had a sharp point, I thought as a hanger nearly poked me in the eye. Working quickly, I crouched down, unraveling the wire as I used to do as a kid. I pulled the two ends together, twisting the rest around the top of the umbrella.

No one found me. I wanted to escape. Run to the next house. Call the police again.

But, my adrenaline rush was fading. I was cold and tired and scared out of my mind. Shivering, I closed my eyes so I could focus on the sounds around me. I didn't move a muscle.

"Hello?"

At the sound of the voice, my eyes shot open and I tightened my grip on the umbrella. Had I been asleep? How much time had passed?

When the closet door opened, I thrust my makeshift weapon at the blinding light. The woman who jumped away from the doorway was wearing the uniform of a local police officer. She spoke into the walkie-talkie on her shoulder.

"I've found her. Bedroom in the rear of the house. Looks like they've done a number on her." She crouched down, extending her hand to me. "It's okay. You can come out now."

"Please. You have to help me. They're trying to kill me."

She nodded. "I know. We found them."

I didn't move. "How? How did you find them?"

A look of sadness passed over her face. "You called us. My friend Kevin lives nearby. Decided to come check on you even though he was off duty. Saw the broken window, called for us to come."

"How did he know my name?"

The woman shook her head. "He didn't. We don't."

"Someone was calling my name."

"When we got here, Kevin was missing. We followed a blood trail to the house next door. Kevin was in the basement beside another young man."

"Clay! Is he okay?"

The officer nodded. "He's on his way to the hospital. But, he's going to be okay. We'd like to bring you there. Get you checked out." She reached out a hand.

I put down my umbrella and allowed her to help me to my feet. She put an arm around my shoulders as she guided me through the house. Red and blue lights flashed in the hallway from the cars in front.

The officer guided me to an ambulance, where a medical technician sat me on a bed and wrapped me in a blanket. He asked my name and if there was a hospital I preferred. I told them I wanted to go where Clay was. Then, I laid down and closed my eyes.

When I opened them again, I was in a hospital bed. I was wearing one of those shifts that were laughingly called gowns and a tube in my hand was connected to a bag of clear liquid hanging over my head.

The officer that had found me in the closet was guarding my

door. When I groaned, she turned around, smiling as she came to stand by the bed.

"Hi, Ellie. Are you feeling any better?"

"Maybe? I'm warm again."

"That's good. You've been asleep for a while. I was hoping you could tell me what happened."

"What part?"

"Why don't you start at the beginning?"

I used the hand without a tube to point to a chair. "You might want to sit down. This is going to take a while."

I could tell she didn't believe me. I watched her type out notes on her phone as I told her about Larkin's bathymetry project. I explained our encounters with Mr. Grumpy and being knocked out of the boat. When I told her about the attack at the campsite, she pulled up the incident report and read through it before having me continue.

It took over an hour for me to explain how I ended up in the neighbor's closet. I offered to pay for the broken window, but the officer just waved her hand dismissively and told me I should get some rest.

I tried, but my mind kept wandering to Clay. The officer couldn't tell me anything. I started badgering the doctors and nurses that came to check on me, but they had no answers either. Finally, the doctor released me.

I changed back into my normal clothes, sitting on the edge of the bed while I waited for my discharge instructions. Someone knocked on the door.

"Come in."

I was expecting to see the nurse. Not Larkin. He scowled as he entered the room.

"Don't think I'm paying you and Mr. Marris for sleeping on the job."

"We're not—"

Larkin smiled. "I'm kidding. How are you, Ellie?"

"I'm . . . what are you doing here?"

"Clay called me. Told me what happened."

"He's okay?"

Larkin nodded. "He's fine. Couple of broken ribs. Doctor wants to keep him another day because he was so dehydrated, but he should be sprung tomorrow."

"So, why are you *here* if he's staying another night?"

"Figured you could probably use a ride. Plus, I wanted to

show you something."

Confused, I took the paper he handed me. I recognized the printout of the map program. It was a depth profile, zoomed in to the northern shore. Larkin pointed where the river fed into the lake.

"I found the *Otter*."

Epilogue

"Why call it dredging?" I asked as Clay and I sat in our kayak in the middle of Elver Lake. We were just outside the orange buoys that separated the lake from the work zone. On the shore were all sorts of heavy machinery and several dumpsters. I turned back to Clay. "Dredging sounds like something cool. They should call it *digging up mud*. Because that's all they're doing."

Clay scooted forward to kiss the top of my head before returning to his seat. "You think Larkin's going to find anything down there?"

"I think Larkin's insane. Swimming where that huge crane is."

"It's not a crane. It's a backhoe. But he's nowhere near where they're working. Besides, there is a light down there. The operator should see him."

I shook my head. Larkin had explained the plan more times than I could count. It didn't mean I understood it any better.

From our perch, I could just barely make out Larkin at the bottom of the lake. In his scuba gear, he reminded me a little too much of the *Lake Monster Torturers*, as they had been dubbed by the local news.

I shook my head, ridding them from my mind. It would be several months before they went to trial. After nearly killing a police officer, it would be a long time before I had to worry about them finding me again.

Clay and I watched Larkin for a long time. He had already done some soil samples to help pinpoint the location of the missing ship. Now that he knew where to look, he was wielding a strange machine that concentrated the water around him into a type of pressure washer, using the spray to dig into the silt at the bottom of the lake.

Eventually, the water became too murky to see. Clay and I rowed back to shore, walking to the worksite. Larkin had set up a table under a pop-up canopy. His graduate student assistant waved to us before grabbing an oxygen tank and swimming back to Larkin.

Clay shook his head. "I don't envy Alex."

I smiled. *"I want to study marine biology. Great. You can swim back and forth and change out my oxygen tank."*

Larkin and his assistant worked long after the dredging crew quit for the day. I was about to suggest Clay and I return to the campsite when Larkin waded out of the water. In his hand, he carried a crate the size of a shoebox.

Clay and I rushed to the table, helping Larkin and Alex to remove their gear. Alex took pictures of the box from all angles before Larkin pried open the top with a crowbar. Inside were dozens of silver forks. I sent Larkin a curious glance.

"I don't get it. I thought the boat was supposed to be full of treasure."

Larkin shrugged. "I'm sure one of those crates will have some gold. The settlers did trade with each other. But, you should see the boat. It's home to some amazing creatures. It's going to take years to study them all."

"But, the guys who captured us. They thought they were going to get rich from what they found."

Larkin shook his head. "Finding this ship? That's treasure enough."

Did you like this story?

Join my newsletter to learn about other new releases.

Mooncrossed
by Ashleigh Stevens

**One space station. Two estranged best friends.
Can romance blossom in space?**

For Captain Jason Tyler, life is good. As one of the best pilots in the fleet, he is selected to run daily transport shuttles to the moon. His charismatic personality and mesmerizing smile charm everyone around him. Except for the one person who matters the most.

Doctor Anika Verde is excited to be named chief medical technician on the new space station orbiting the moon. Being six hours away from the nearest hospital gives frontier medicine a new meaning. Unfortunately, she's going to need some help.

Once upon a time, Anika and Tyler were inseparable. Now, she can't stand to be in the same room as him and he has no idea why.

Missing medical supplies, construction accidents, and deadly viruses force these former friends to work together. With such a tangled history, Anika and Tyler must determine whether they can put aside their differences or remain forever mooncrossed.

Prologue

Tyler

"On behalf of the faculty, administration, and staff of the International Space Endeavor, it is my pleasure to welcome you to the ISE Academy's fourteenth annual commencement. This year, eight new pilots will join our fleet, along with six flight technicians, two station engineers . . ."

I looked down at the tablet I had propped on the back of the chair in front of me. Since I wasn't wearing my hearing aids, I had turned on the automatic captioning. Technically, if I were looking at him, I would be able to understand Andrew Westinghouse without the tablet. His microphone was at a volume within my hearing range and he glanced my way often enough that I could read his lips. But, it was much more fun to watch the translations.

. . . Four nuance eating three . . .

Beside me, my roommate tapped me on the shoulder. Jesse pointed to my tablet and sent me a quizzical look. I just shook my head as I signed my response.

I'll explain later.

Watching the horrible captions helped make the dull speech by the ISE founder more endurable. Every so often, I would look back towards the speaker to make sure I wasn't missing anything important.

"As you are aware, I founded ISE back in 2050, when the United States, Japan, China, and the European Union simultaneously decided to completely defund their space exploration programs."

Yeah, of course I knew that. Everyone graduating did. And I

was willing to bet all the people gathered to here to watch the ceremony knew as well. I turned back to my tablet.

But as Westinghouse droned on, even the captions lost their novelty. The heat and humidity were too unbearable to pay attention to a boring speech. I watched the guy in front of me pull at the collar of his uniform. The girl next to him had beads of sweat dripping down the back of her neck. I resisted the urge to wipe my own.

The faculty were seated on risers behind Westinghouse. My boss was among them. Argo's bald head was shining in the summer sun. He looked nearly as bored as me. He kept glancing to his left.

To the travelport. Where shuttles were taking off and landing like clockwork. Some were heading to other travelports across the world. One was most likely heading to Gagarin, the space station named after the first person to orbit the Earth. Beyond the travelport, I could see the towering skyscrapers of New York City.

Suddenly, everyone around me started cheering. I turned to Jesse.

Is it time to march?

Jesse shook his head. *Westinghouse just announced a second resort.*

I glanced at my screen. Miraculously, the captioning had worked, although I had to scroll up slightly to read it all. *Thanks to two members of this triumvirate class, I am pleased to announce that dream is becoming a reality.*

Everyone was looking around. I tried to avoid making eye contact with anyone. Three seats to my left, my best friend caught my eye. Anika gave a small smirk before returning her attention to the podium.

Westinghouse was smiling like the cat who swallowed the canary. "Four short years ago, each of you completed a Business 101 course prior to entering the Academy. One student among you designed a revolutionary new type of solar panel. When combined with the shuttle designs of another student, JT Designs was born. Over the last four years, this company has developed a new fleet of ships that are faster and more efficient than anything ISE has created to date. With these new shuttles, we can now make it to the moon in six hours."

A murmur went through the crowd. A fellow pilot sitting in front of me turned around.

"Six hours! Can you imagine?"

Jesse balked, a hint of Southern twang in his voice. "I'll believe it when I see it."

I elbowed the co-founder of JT Designs, signing so no one could overhear us. *You have seen it. The prototype was finished last week.*

Oh man! Jesse closed his eyes with a satisfied smile. *She was FAST. I bet I could make her faster.* He opened his eyes. *If you just streamlined her a little more—*

I elbowed him again as Westinghouse held up a hand for silence. He gave us the highlights of the project timeline. But, despite the technology, it would take nearly a decade before they would be able to break ground on the new resort.

Finally, it was time to march across the stage to receive our diplomas. I followed my roommate to the queue at the base of the steps.

"Ryan Sweet, Security. Morgan Taylor, Communications. Captain Jesse Townsend, Pilot. Captain Jason Tyler, Pilot."

I marched to the center of the stage, where Argo pinned wings to my lapel and shook my hand. Then Westinghouse handed me my diploma.

I returned to my seat to watch the final few names. When "Doctor Anika Verde, Medicine and Counseling" was announced, Jesse and I cheered and whistled. Anika tried to glare at us as one of her professors pinned a caduceus to her lapel. But I could see the gleam in her eyes. She had been waiting for this day for a long time.

After a few more closing remarks, the ceremony was finally over. Jesse gave Anika a huge congratulatory hug before running to find his mother and grandmother. I went to stand with my best friend.

She was looking mournfully at the main building of the Academy. "I can't believe it's over."

I put my arm around her shoulders and squeezed her tight. I flashed her my famous smile. "No it's not. It's just the beginning."

Anika shook her head. "I'm going to be up on Gagarin. You and Jesse are going to be doing shuttle runs. I'm going to miss seeing you guys every day."

I shrugged. "You heard Westinghouse. You, me, Jesse? We're the triumvirate. Nothing can keep us apart."

I wish I knew then how wrong I was.

Chapter 1

Anika

This morning, I realized how much I truly missed my kitchen. Not the one in my last apartment, but the one in my house back home, where I used to help my mother make pancakes when I was little.

I came to this realization when I sat down to *breakfast* and was served the reheated ready-to-eat substance that was being called a bagel. In reality, it was a round brick with a hole in the center that would not even be fit to use as a hockey puck.

Nevertheless, I smiled as I took my first bite of the dry, dense donut, quickly hiding my distaste with a large swig of water. Captain Valerie was trying graciously to be a good hostess. It was not her fault that her cargo vessel did not contain a true kitchen. It was not her fault that she was provided with enough field rations to last several months, not the one week her voyage was scheduled to take. After three days of prepared meals, I was craving real food.

I studied Captain Valerie while I tried to chew and swallow the sawdust in my mouth. The drink of water made the substance even more difficult to masticate. She poured some steaming water into a mug of instant coffee, then folded her long, slender body into her Captain's chair.

When she swiveled to face her cockpit, her pale blonde hair fell in soft waves just below her shoulders. Over the past few days, however, I had come to learn that her social skills were very limited, probably a result of spending so much time hauling cargo without much company. Her relief captain, a student doing a correspondence semester, spent more time in her cabin sending transmissions to her friends than interacting with us.

Captain Valerie turned back to me, nodding her head

towards the window. "There it is, Doc."

I followed her gaze to see our destination ahead. Although the ten-story cube was smaller than my previous assignment, it was still a monstrosity. In the nearly nine years I had spent living on Gagarin, I had never failed to appreciate its beauty. However, even though Gagarin was more massive and elegant, Anders-Borman-Lovell was by far the more impressive station. For, while the larger, older station orbited the elegant, enduring Earth, the newer, smaller station orbited the mysterious, majestic moon.

Captain Valerie's voice brought me back to the shuttle. "We dock today. Looking forward to getting off this rust bucket?"

I finally managed to swallow my bagel. I took another large gulp of water before answering Captain Valerie's question.

"It's not that bad. Been a long three days, though."

"I know. I'm looking forward to spending some time with my boyfriend."

There weren't many people living at the new station and I had a feeling I knew whom she was anxious to meet. I sent her a curious look. "You're seeing someone on ABL?"

Her bright blue eyes twinkled with excitement. "One of the pilots."

I tried to not to roll my eyes. According to yesterday's staff meeting, which I was able to attend remotely, there were three pilots currently on the station, one of whom would probably depart before we arrived. I had little doubt she was seeing one of my least favorite people, but I held my tongue. Thankfully, Captain Valerie changed the subject.

"Are you excited about your new assignment?"

"I am. Working at Gagarin was fun, interacting with all the tourists, but this is exciting, too. It's like frontier medicine. We're three days away from the nearest hospital."

"Plus no annoying tourists."

I smiled. "In my previous position, my boss detested the tourists. He attended to the station staff and left everyone else to us underlings. It was amazing what trouble they could get into. I had one man come in full of bruises. His nose was bloody and broken, so were four of his ribs, and he had a mild concussion. I assumed he had gotten into a bar fight. You know what he said when I asked what happened?

Captain Valerie shook her head.

"He didn't see the need for his safety harness in the shuttle. When the pilot tried to match the station's rotation in order to dock, he was tossed like a rag doll."

Captain Valerie laughed. "That's one of the reasons I chose cargo over passenger shuttles. Tourists can be really stupid." She sighed. "I can't imagine living out here. I thought about applying, but it's not for me. My boyfriend told me they have to shuttle people back and forth every day. One day off out of every four. I like my job better. Three days of quiet, hauling cargo by myself, a day at the new station to hang out, three quiet days back, and a day at the old station to rest. Watch tourists. Maybe visit my family and friends. You guys are all alone."

I gave a noncommittal shrug as I tried to finish my breakfast. One of the best advantages of the new stations was that I would be working with one of my best friends.

The first time I had met Jesse Townsend, I was sitting at a table in the Academy cafeteria, only a few weeks into my first semester at the school. I was eating lunch while studying for an anatomy exam, trying to read the book on my communications tablet and my study notes on my research tablet. I was memorizing the different types of cells when Ellie's face popped onto my screen. With a sigh, I accepted the study break as I waved a greeting to the holographic image of my pseudosister.

I moved my tablet so I could better see her miniature projection frantically lamenting about her latest breakup. Both her parents were Deaf and Ellie had been born with a slight hearing impairment that became more profound as she grew older. At twenty-two, Ellie's hearing aid no longer helped her to hear words, only background noise, and she preferred to go without, relying mostly on American Sign Language as her primary form of communication. Since my father was Deaf and my mother always signed, I was also fluent in both English and ASL.

I did my best to reassure Ellie that she would eventually find her soul mate. However, I was distracted by the guy staring at me from the next table. His eyes, the color of a tropical ocean, were watching me intensely as Ellie and I held our silent conversation.

When I finally managed to end the transmission, I rearranged my tablets so I could resume studying for my exam, but before I could open my files, he came to sit at my table. His lean, muscular six-foot-two body was dressed in the olive-gray shirt and khaki slacks required of all flying students. The badge on his lapel indicated he was in his first year. His sandy hair stood straight up, about three inches above his head in a flat top. Since this hairstyle had become the trend of most of flying students in our class, it had been dubbed the *pilot's cut.*

The guy was tan, as if he had spent his summer on the beach, not here in New York. I later learned that his tan was a result of running track at his Georgia high school. When he spoke, his voice revealed just a hint of Southern twang.

"Hi." He glanced at my brick-red shirt and khaki uniform skirt. "I, uh, know greys aren't supposed to fraternize with reds, but I wanted to ask ya a question."

I smiled at the joke, since socialization between departments was actually highly encouraged. As I nodded for him to proceed, I prepared myself for the inevitable medical pickup line.

"Can ya teach me to sign?"

My smile faltered and my face must have taken on a look of surprise. I had been expecting the *Will you play doctor with me* line I had heard nearly every day since arriving at the college.

The guy noticed my confusion and continued with a hurried explanation. "Ya see, my roommate signs like that to his tablet and I kinda want to learn it. If we're going to be flying together, I want to be able to communicate with him. But I don't think he'd make a great teacher. He gets annoyed when I ask too many questions. But, you're in the medical program, so you need a lot of patience."

At first, I thought he meant *patients*, creating a bad joke. I scowled, figuring he had just taken the long route to a bad pickup line, and he quickly continued his monologue.

"Okay, so maybe you don't have a lot of patience, yet, but you need to practice your patience and you can practice on me and then you'll have enough patience to deal with your patients."

He paused as he considered what he had just uttered. "Oh. That came out wrong. Lemme start over. My name is Jesse and I noticed you know sign language. I would like to learn. Do ya think you could teach me?"

In the coming months, I would learn that I would be the only person to ever see that shy, embarrassed side of Jesse, who usually has such a confident air about him. As I watched him repeatedly lifting a drink bottle, only to put it down without reaching his lips, I welcomed the opportunity to teach Jesse and I invited him for what would become a weekly silent supper. Every Sunday evening, I would make us dinner, since I love to cook, and we would spend the entire evening communicating in only ASL. We learned a lot about each other and he quickly became one of my best friends.

Nearly an hour after my first glimpse of the lunar station, I was standing at the cargo door, ready to disembark. My few pieces of luggage would be unloaded by the cargo room attendants and delivered to my quarters. Meanwhile, Captain Valerie would monitor the offloading of her vessel. In addition to the food, clothing, and other supplies requested by the permanent and temporary workers on the station, the shuttle also carried the construction materials necessary to begin the lunar resort project. The cargo attendants would spend the next several hours removing the load from the ship, storing it in the massive two-storied cargo hold at the base of the cube.

I was met at the airlock by a young man wearing khaki pants and the pumpkin-orange shirt of a communications student. He introduced himself and said he was to bring me to the staff meeting room. I followed him into the lift, carrying a small bag containing some personal items and my communication tablet.

During the short ride, my escort reminded me of the layout of the station, which I had memorized before leaving Gagarin. While he did this in a friendly, tour-guide manner, I got the impression his motivation had more to do with the hope he would not have to continue to serve as my guide for the remainder of the day.

We exited on Deck Seven and I could see my infirmary on the left. However, we turned right, instead entering the administrative offices home to the communications and operations departments. I followed my guide along a windy corridor to a small conference room, where Director Kimura had already begun the daily briefing with the senior staff members. My escort beckoned me inside, where I stood just over the threshold, observing the woman standing with her back to me as she addressed the table.

Kimura was petite, about five feet tall, with black hair reaching her waist. Her gold uniform shirt indicated that she had been a security officer before becoming director of the station. At the director's right, Sonia Menendez, director of station communications, donned an orange uniform shirt, her dark eyes fixed intensely on the director. The chief engineer, Ito Chen sat on the director's other side. He was shorter than I had imagined, his chocolate brown uniform making him appear even more diminutive. Sitting beside Ito, silently drumming his fingers along the table, sat the chief of security, Malcolm Palmer. His muscular frame stretched his gold uniform, and his blonde hair was cut so short, he almost looked bald.

Captain Tyler sat beside Malcolm, quietly signing across the table to Jesse, who looked just as good as he had when we first met in the Academy cafeteria. I watched their conversation for a while, curious to know what could be more interesting than the meeting, raising my eyebrows when I realized Jesse was interpreting Director Kimura's words for his roommate.

Examining Captain Tyler more closely, I was surprised to see he was sporting a nice summer tan. I wondered how had he managed to do that in January while running passengers from New York to Gagarin and back. His blue eyes twinkled mischievously as he watched Jesse's hands, occasionally asking a question in return. His brown hair was sporting the still-popular pilot's cut, making it easy for me to see his ears.

He turned his attention towards Director Kimura, catching my eye instead. He sent me that cocky smile of his that made women swoon, but instead filled me with anger. We had only spoken a handful of times the last few years, always with Jesse as a mediator, despite our complicated history.

Instead of returning his smile, I simply glared at him, hooking my index finger behind my ear. It was the sign for *hearing aid* and I knew immediately he understood my question, since he refused to acknowledge me and returned his gaze to Jesse. Frowning, I paid closer attention to the director's discussion of the construction crew.

"The crew arrives Sunday. If Doc ever arrives—" She interrupted herself when she saw Captain Tyler's raised hand. "What is it, Ty?"

He simply pointed in my direction and everyone turned to face me.

Chapter 2

Tyler

"Sorry I'm late," Anika apologized. She briskly walked to the empty chair beside Jesse. He gave her a quick hug. As she settled into her seat, I couldn't help but think how run down she looked.

Sure, everyone else probably saw her Dr. Verde facade: the petite, confident young woman who had managed to earn dual medical degrees and be the chief medical technician by the age of thirty. And, man, she looked hot in that uniform. She was the only person I knew who elected to wear a black knee-length skirt instead of slacks like the rest of us. It definitely worked for her.

But, I saw past all that. Her chestnut hair was falling out of its red tie. Did she even realize she was absently tucking it behind her ears? Then, there were her brown eyes. The weariness I saw told me she hadn't had a decent night's sleep in forever.

Maybe I was simply projecting. After all, when was the last time I had slept through the night? But, her skin. Although she was normally pale, today she looked nearly transparent. It was as if she hadn't seen the sun in months. Knowing her, she had probably locked herself away on Gagarin. I wondered when she last visited home.

Anika caught me watching her and sent me an angry look before turning away. She had been doing that for the past five years. It didn't even bother me anymore. It was so good to see her. I was excited to be working with her. Suddenly, it hit me.

I really missed you, I signed.

Unfortunately, Director Kimura had just asked Anika a question. All eyes but mine had been looking at one of the two women, so thankfully no one saw my confession.

"I haven't been to the infirmary, yet." Anika was signing as she spoke, probably for my benefit, though she refused to look in my direction. "I'm hoping everything I requested has been delivered. I'm going to do inventory today and make sure I know where everything is. Then, I'm going to review all the medical files. Everyone is supposed to have had evaluations within the past six months. Both physical *and* mental." She sent a knowing glance around the room.

I followed her gaze. More than one person shrank back, looking anywhere but at the doctor. When Anika caught my eye, I gave her my famous smile and wiggled my eyebrows. She simply glared at me. Maybe she already figured out that my evaluations were overdue. She looked back at Kimura as she continued.

"After all that, I want to start going over emergency protocols. I'm assuming that there are plans in place for injuries on the surface?"

Director Kimura shrugged. "The site supervisor arrives in a few days with the crew. The company may have some emergency plans. But, we, as a station, do not."

Anika's eyes narrowed. "The moon is about to become a major construction site."

Uh oh! I recognized that body language. I could just barely hear the tone of voice that usually accompanied it. It was the one Anika saved for when someone seriously messes up. I'd lost track how often I had heard it. Usually in my direction.

"There are going to be accidents. What happens when a beam falls and crushes someone? We need protocols. At the very least, I'm going to need someone with medical training. Someone on the surface to handle the emergency from the beginning and assist me when the patient returns to the station."

Director Kimura frowned. "Do you have anyone in mind?"

"Why not the site supervisor?" asked Jesse.

Anika shook her head. "The supervisor rotates every four weeks. I don't want to have to train a new assistant every month. And, frankly, I need someone who understands medical terminology. I don't have time to explain myself in a life-or-death situation." Anika pursed her lips as she sighed. "I'll figure something out."

I could see the wheels had already started turning.

Want to read more?
Mooncrossed is now available at your favorite digital bookstore!

About the Author

Once upon a time, there was a girl who loved reading and learning so much that she wanted to share her writing with others. She wrote her first novella at twelve-years-old, although it has never been published. She continued writing for the next twenty years, developing a writing style and finding a comfortable genre.

In 2010, just before the birth of her first child, Ashleigh decided to publish her first novel. Not long after, Ashleigh decided to become a stay-at-home mother in order to spend time with her daughter and continue her writing.

Currently, Ashleigh lives in Southern Connecticut with her husband and her four beautiful children, whom she homeschools. In her spare time, Ashleigh continues working on her novels, hoping to publish more soon.

Read more at www.AshleighStevensBSB.com